GIRL
gets
GHOSTED

GIRL gets GHOSTED

a lesbian romance novella

WAVERLY DECKER

Calhoun Howard
New York, New York

Girl Gets Ghosted
Copyright © 2023 by Waverly Decker
Excerpt from *The 30-Day Engagement*
copyright © 2022 by Waverly Decker
All rights reserved.

Cover photo © auleena/Shutterstock.com
Back cover photo © pixelshot/Canva.com
Cover © 2023 Calhoun Howard LLC

For information about this book, rights inquiries, and for permission to use portions of this book other than for review purposes, contact
Calhoun Howard LLC
2248 Broadway #1330
New York, NY 10024
permissions@calhounhoward.com

The publisher is not responsible for websites that
are not owned by the publisher.

Library of Congress Control Number: 2023934696
ISBNs: 979-8-9866210-5-0 (paperback), 979-8-9866210-3-6 (ebook)

calhounhoward.com

First Edition: October 2023

10 9 8 7 6 5 4 3 2 1

one

Autumn was Charlize's favorite season of the year, bar none. It meant the crackle of dry leaves under her bicycle wheels, and hot cider, and warm spice in teacups. It meant the crisp smell of apple peels mixed with wood smoke and rain. She loved the way that brisk air crept in around her collar and cuffs to lift her mood, and loved wrapping a scarf around her neck to stop the draft. She reveled in the ever-shortening days, and in the prospect of outdoor activities like bonfires that didn't end with her skin in a state of extreme sunburn. Summer was a monochrome harsh yellow, and fall was a riotous kaleidoscope.

Of course, she *also* loved that the arrival of autumn meant that the end-of-summer rush of students returning to school was over, and that she could end her work shift as associate housing director of Chestnut College at a reasonable hour. Everyone who needed a home away from home was settled in—provided they wanted that home to be a dorm room—and all but the most attentive of parents had ceased daily checks on their children's whereabouts and happiness (and calling any campus extension that would pick up when their numbers flashed across the ID panel).

Charlize's office was quiet. She could attend to the growing pile of work requests, put together her inventory report for the upcoming department meeting where they were slated to discuss "the future of student furniture," and see about getting a teetering pyramid of microwave/refrigerator combos repaired and out of the basement closet at resident services.

But all of that could wait for another day. At five o'clock sharp, Charlize slung her messenger bag over her shoulder, strapped on her helmet, and went down the broad stone steps of the resident services building to unlock her bike for the commute home. She'd hardly pedaled a block when she saw the one thing that she *hated* about autumn. Her *enemy*. Her *nemesis*.

A candlelit pumpkin in a dorm room window.

Charlize slammed on the brakes and waited for an oncoming car to pass, then made a left across the street to Oak dorm. "They *know* better," she said, not even trying to keep her voice muted as her tires squeaked on the damp pavement. "There's a memorial in the foyer, even." Oak Hall's bike racks were around the back of the building, and she'd have to come all the way around again to use her employee badge and get in through the front, so Charlize decided to do things her way. She rode straight to the first-floor window where the pumpkin grimaced—definitely a candle and not a realistic LED—and banged on the sill.

The windowpane slid up. "Uh, *hell*-o, where have you been all my life?" asked the gangly sophomore or junior. Both were eligible to live in Oak, according to the housing rules, though usually only juniors got in, since the dorm's location close to the center of campus allowed for maximum sleep time before morning classes.

The young man who leered from inside struck Charlize as the sort who preferred maximum sleep while ensuring everyone else got the minimum. She could see an oversized sound system behind him and a cluster of partygoers sitting on the speakers.

"For the last decade of your life, I've been working in resident services," she answered calmly, though her fingers on her handlebars were slick with sweat. The student's visitors whistled and heckled him from the dimly lit background. "So I regret to inform you of the rule I'm sure your RA has passed along and that you read when you signed your housing contract for this year. No fire, flame, or smoke in the dorms. You can have jack-o-lanterns on the steps of Oak and on the outer edge of the path on the lawn, on the thirty-first only, or you can bring them to the campus carving contest on Saturday night."

The younger man groaned. "Aw, come on. Look how good we decorated Oak! These are the finishing touch. The pièce de résistance, if you will." That earned him a giggle from the party.

Charlize had to admit that Oak's Halloween decorations were legitimately impressive. A pair of giant skeletons stretched a net over the entrance in their bony hands, and a cluster of spiders dangled menacingly from the webbing. Almost every window of the dorm displayed a cutout of a leaf, or a black cat, or a crow. But she hated Halloween, partly because she didn't like the aesthetic and partly because she hated how the holiday so often gifted her with work problems. She'd always tried to ignore the decorations policies when she could, because when she'd been a student, she'd been on probation—*probation!*—for hanging a poster of Katniss Everdeen on her room's door and violating the fire code.

She shook her head, ready to reply. One of the characters hidden in the shadows of the dorm room said something about an "evil old witch." Another whispered something even ruder, and Charlize's brain filled in "needs to get fucked," which was gross...and also true, not that it was any of their business. She'd heard enough of this kind of shit over the years. Usually it rolled off, but not this time. She was *mad*.

Charlize didn't care about the decorations. She cared about the ghosts.

"A girl died in Oak. When I was a student. You walk past the plaque every time you come home." Charlize had been a freshman, and had showed up to school a week early to memorize the campus map and start her work-study job in the housing department. She'd walked fellow freshman Bayli Dilley to her room in Oak Hall, sprayed graphite into her sticky lock, waved when they passed in the cafeteria. And then Bayli had fallen asleep with a candle burning. Charlize shook her head to push away the memory.

"No fire," she repeated. "House rules. Get an LED candle. They've got them in the bookstore." She huffed in a breath and blew out the flame, then pushed herself off the stone side of the building with one muddy foot and pedaled back to the street. Her shoe's half-print wouldn't last long; a light mist was clinging to her windbreaker. But it would last long enough for her to email the Oak resident advisor in the morning and ask them to check that the marked room was in compliance.

There had been a second fire in the intervening years since Bayli's passing. Fortunately, that one, Charlize's first year as regular staff, had only wiped out a full floor of student belongings when the newly installed sprinkler system did its assigned job. Charlize shivered. There wouldn't be any tragedies on her watch.

She'd take care of the students. The ghosts, too.

☾

CHARLIZE HAD A TEN-MINUTE ride to her building, mostly down a tree-lined street populated by young families, professionals, and a few retired folks—and, thankfully, none of Chestnut College's students, faculty, or staff, as far as she knew. Her apartment was one of a half-dozen in what had once been a grand house, and later segmented into residences that would be cramped to share, but were perfectly cozy for one person. She locked her bike to the porch railing and went inside to pet her doggo, a four-year-old rescue she'd named Licorice that was one part black lab, two parts mutt.

"Hey, baby, I'm here," Charlize called, though it was unnecessary. After-work scritches and hugs were what Licorice lived for. He was always waiting the moment Charlize came home.

Home sweet home, decorated with the finest furniture Chestnut College had ever discarded. The couch was her secret favorite, not to mention her biggest secret, as she'd found it next to the dumpster behind Elm dorm when she was a senior and rolled it off campus on her skateboard. She'd never been entirely certain that the couch was *trash*; it was clean and in good shape, and had held up nicely in the six years since she'd graduated, even with Licorice playing tug atop its cushions. The other resident services staff might have been able to tell her the provenance, but her colleagues were all at least a decade older, and they didn't socialize with Charlize outside of work—and definitely didn't socialize with Charlize at her apartment.

That was probably for the best. She didn't want to have to buy a slipcover to hide her youthful transgression.

Autumn was when she felt the most sociable, though, and more and more Charlize wished someone *would* come over. One of her childhood neighbors, Erika, was the mom-friend at the center of a small galaxy of friends held together since college by a group chat, and they'd all met up in Boston over Labor Day weekend. But the last few weeks had been busy, especially for Bliss, their remote member who lived in New York, and when they got together, it was almost never at Charlize's place. Their meetups were sliding from monthly to quarterly to...rarely.

That was growing up, she supposed. Her own "flirty thirty" was coming soon. Charlize grabbed Licorice's leash and sent a message to the chat.

> Charlize Horse: What's going on this weekend
>
> Erika: Fall fundraiser!
>
> blissfulmess: Park Slope Halloween Parade, we're a sponsor this year.
>
> meowsville: work party for kitten adoption event coming up next week
>
> goofbot2000: Interviewing seven potential roommates, wish me luck

Solo tonight, then. Charlize put her phone in her pocket and let Licorice tug her outside for a stroll around the block. Licorice preferred to do his business first, pleasure later, so it was well after sunset before they had sniffed all the trees and grass and decided on the best peeing spot before coming back to the golden glow of the porch light.

Back inside, Charlize poured a bowl of kibble for Licorice and, in solidarity, a bowl of Cocoa Puffs for herself. She leaned against the counter, spooning cereal into her mouth and listening to Licorice's crunches and snuffles. It was...nice. Homey.

Still...

Charlize headed for the living room and her illicit couch. Feet up on the coffee table, she flipped channels aimlessly. Thursday night television was pretty meh. She wasn't in the mood for the Halloween specials she'd seen so many times before. Licorice jumped onto the couch and curled against her hip. She rubbed behind his ears, right where he liked it. Licorice would always come find her on the couch.

But if she was being honest, nobody else was going to.

She turned off the television and pulled out her phone, then went searching for apps to install. Her. OkCupid. Tinder. CoffeeCupLuv. A few more that she'd previously uninstalled out of pure laziness—easier to let her profile go stale than to go through the deletion process on the websites.

Licorice snored at her side as she flipped through profiles. She recognized a couple of women who'd ghosted her last year. Swipe. Left, left, left. *Taker, not a giver. I don't read my messages, DM me on my social profile. Just here to have fun. Fit only.* A handful of TERFs. And then: *No dogs.*

All bad vibes people, as her friend Bliss would say. She was done with the fruitless exploration after two apps.

Charlize levered herself off the couch to get ready for bed. Her jeans and sweater went in the hamper in the bathroom, and she put on the tank and boxers she wore as pajamas. Then the rest of her bedtime routine: Brush teeth. Floss. Rub zit cream over her pale white skin and freckles. Run hands over her short, tousled red hair, and—two years after it was cut—reach for the elastic ponytail holder she didn't need anymore out of habit. And, finally, the question she'd asked the mirror every night since: *Who are you today?*

When she'd first cut her hair, and gone home for winter break, her dad had joked that she wanted to be a boy since she shaved her head and dressed in a T-shirt and jeans with—well, she hadn't found the right shoes yet. He hadn't bothered to ask what he really wanted to know, so she kept questioning herself, just to be sure.

Boys or girls? People in general, gender aside? *Girls—definitely girls. Women.* And if her dad thought she looked like an overgrown teen boy on the outside, she was pretty sure she felt like a woman on the inside. She resented the question her dad hadn't asked, but it was good to check in, she supposed, to find the piece of her that came in orange and pink stripes and was *gay, gay, gay.*

She could figure out the rest of the labels later.

Charlize crawled into bed, and Licorice, tags jingling, came into the room and circled three times before flopping down on the dog bed she'd bought for him when it was clear he preferred the floor. "Even you, bud? Gotta rub it in that I'm sleeping alone tonight?"

Licorice *woofed* softly, and Charlize laughed. "It's okay. I respect your preferences." If only everybody would do the same. She started uninstalling the dating apps, but when Licorice yawned, she did too. "And I respect your reminders." She plugged in her phone and set it on the nightstand. "Maybe I'll meet someone real tomorrow."

There was no answer except soft doggie snores. Charlize turned out the light.

two

ON FRIDAY MORNING, KYLA DAVIS logged into her work account and filled out her time card with five straight days of vacation. Her PTO balance was low. She could take one more week, and then she'd have to be back on a regular schedule at her job, strategizing social media initiatives from nine to five—and teaching herself software development after hours.

Her manager had been enthusiastic about Kyla taking time off to "increase her knowledge of technology and apply that to her current role," and—unspoken—running out her vacation days so that when the winter holidays came around, Kyla would be the one covering the office for everyone else. Kyla hadn't dared admit that her real goal was a new job. She was sick of bots and reply guys and trying to keep up with every last meme, every last popular music snippet, and the intricacies of today's slang versus yesterday's, all while balancing her employer's desire to be known as a serious purveyor of software solutions (but the kind of serious purveyor who you'd want to have a beer with). Whatever joy she'd once found in selecting the perfect GIF was long gone. She didn't dare hope for more than coasting through the next few years.

Kyla also hadn't dared tell her family that she was burning through her time off and likely wouldn't be home for Thanksgiving. Or Christmas. Or watching the ball drop on New Year's Eve with champagne and her mother's famous snack tray, guaranteed to be no more than crumbs at midnight. It would all be worth it, she reasoned, if she could make the jump from typing text into an app to creating the code behind one.

Skipping family time was stress for a later day, so she bundled up for a quick walk to the Isabella Stewart Gardner Museum and spent an hour exploring the gardens. A little greenery as fall turned everything shades of bronze and gold soothed her racing, anxious mind. On the way home, she bought a giant coffee from Dunkin', which felt like the right fuel for the afternoon ahead.

She was going to finish an app. It was time for do or die.

Back at her desk, wrapped in a fleece blanket, with a cinnamon-scented candle and her coffee within arm's reach, Kyla looked through her list of half-finished projects. She needed to put some more code up on GitHub soon, but mostly, she wanted to get at least one app into a shape worth sharing. There was a half-finished project that she hoped could interface with social media, email, calendars, and project management tools to create a personalized to-do list; she wasn't entirely sure how to get that working on the back end. She'd also started the design for a similar standalone personal planner that used AI to turn your task list into an optimized to-do list, including estimated time and resources to complete the work. That one was merely pretty, not functional. Her *ideas* were good. But her coding skills weren't.

Yet.

Finally, she settled on her oldest, and most complete, project: an app called Disaster Date. (Flip, but fair.) "Who hasn't been on at least one of those?" she mumbled to herself as she opened the file folder on her desktop. "Can't blame me when your date turns out just like I told you it would."

Disaster Date was the result of a brainstorming session about what she liked doing (communicating) and what she enjoyed in her current job (bringing people together). She'd worked through a plan, step by step, repurposing code, taking any chance she had to ask for advice, until she had an app that would help people match up—and maybe even have dates that *weren't* disasters.

Hopefully. She didn't quite understand what all the code was doing. Most of it had been written with the help of artificial intelligence, and not all of it made sense to her. But she loved solving problems.

Especially her own.

And her lack of dates, disaster or otherwise, was starting to be a problem.

Disaster Date opened full screen, per her settings. The app was in better shape than she remembered after leaving it to languish for nearly a year. The user interface was clean and cute, courtesy of her tour of duty making graphics for social media. She'd managed a few features she was truly proud of, like interactive icons to express different kinds of interest in a match. A little steaming mug suggested getting together for tea or coffee. There was a fishing rod for the other end of the spectrum, because some people were only looking for a hookup. Seasonal images for fun activities needed work; she'd finished spring and summer, but fall and winter needed to be tested. Kyla changed the testing status to live and clicked the image of a round, white circle. A pop-up appeared. "Wanna build a snowman?"

What the hell. Let's do this. Kyla was ready for prime time. A few clicks and she was releasing her creation to the world, each store proclaiming that Disaster Date was in beta, provided as-is while under development, and for the moment, *free*. Who didn't like free?

Then she freaked out. Kyla blew out the candle. She ran from the cloud of cinnamon-scented smoke to her bedroom and crawled under the duvet. A pillow came under with her, acting as a tentpole for her protective fort.

She set a timer on her phone for fifteen minutes. That was enough invisible time. When the alarm went off, she'd be ready to face the world again.

Kyla opened a meditation app and selected a deep breathing exercise with shaking hands. There was nothing to feel *anxious* about. Nobody was coming to get her. Her app had a million disclaimers on it—*no guarantees your date won't be a disaster*. And the app name set expectations right up front. And she'd done her duty of care, forcing new users through a series of reminders. *Meet in a public place. Exercise caution. Leave if something feels off.*

"Inhale four, hold four, out four, hold four. Inhale."

Forget *you just did the thing* for four.

Exhale.

Kyla's phone chimed gently. Fifteen minutes—and she did feel better. She eased herself back into the world before returning to her desk. Bathroom break. Hair up in a messy bun. Fuzzy socks.

Settled in, she poked the button to turn her multiple monitors back on, and watched, in real time, as Disaster Date got its first download and gained its first member: *Charlize Horse.*

Yes.

Before her eyes, Charlize Horse worked through—Kyla watched as the information filled—*her* profile. Pizza and a movie. Spicy chai. Softball, biking, science and history museums (not art museums, Kyla noted). Then a photo: short red hair. Freckles. A square jaw and sharp nose, a goofy grin that Kyla liked immediately.

One. She had *one* user!

Which meant—

Kyla gasped. There wasn't anybody for Charlize Horse to match with, which was a *bad user experience*. What if she left a review? A *one*-star review? A one-star review *with explanatory text* about what was wrong with Disaster Date? Kyla scrolled up and down the profile, relieved that Charlize Horse had, at least, chosen to see her "match of the day" instead of everyone. And...yes, there, in the "open to dating" section—

Charlize Horse was, theoretically, open to dating Kyla.

Kyla flipped frantically through her test profiles. Her latest, KyLAUGH, was mostly complete. There was a picture that she'd taken on a laundry Saturday, cat-eye glasses peeking out from her beanie, hair in a long blonde braid with curls escaping but tucked up where no one could see, flannel hanging open over a tank top. It was a lazy day look, but anybody who wouldn't want to hang out on a lazy day wasn't worth Kyla's time. She switched to her second monitor, turning some of the buttons on the profile pages on and off, and made sure to activate the smiling summer sunshine icon, even though it wasn't very seasonal this time of year. When she refreshed Charlize Horse's profile, the sunshine showed up.

She took a deep breath. "Here goes nothing." When she clicked the sunshine, it glowed and a pair of sunglasses appeared over its smile. Deep in the backend, she found the option to turn on the daily matches algorithm, which, with only two active site users, would make her Charlize Horse's match of the day. Charlize Horse would get an email and a push alert within the hour.

Until then, Kyla decided to give out her best possible user experience. This match had to feel like a good one, at least until a better one came along. She clicked the sunshine graphic under Charlize Horse's profile photo. "Hey, cutie. Hi there," she whispered. Then she put her hands behind her head and her feet up on her desk. "Let's see if this is a trick or a real treat."

three

Charlize had her feet up on her desk—a desk she'd rescued from a faculty apartment three years ago that was in great shape, except for some dog bite dents on the left front leg, and that was the reason she'd saved it. Some little pupper had made its mark. People went on vacations to see ancient Roman graffiti, and in the present, Charlize was preserving evidence of how humanity, or dogmanity, had lived for future generations. Someday, someone would dig this desk out of the trash and think of the canine who'd applied teeth to its wood.

Her colleagues had filtered out of the office already, and it was, loathsomely, her turn to stay late, even though there was rarely a major problem for the office on a Friday night, even this close to Halloween. No; the problems would come in tomorrow, after the parties and revelry, and then the next day as embarrassed students finally reported what was broken. In the meantime, she had an hour to kill before the phones forwarded directly to maintenance and she could bike home a free woman. Maybe pick up some candy on the way in case any kids came by to trick or treat over the weekend.

It would be nice if someone came by.

She flipped through her phone. The battery was low, but it would hold until she could plug it in at her apartment. The home screen was a mess of icons and blank spaces representing what she had uninstalled. There was still one dating app that she hadn't deleted over the course of the day: Disaster Date.

What a stupid name. Why did I bother? Charlize dragged the app toward the trash bin, but let go before dumping it in. "Ah, why not?" she asked her empty office. "Who doesn't love a good disaster?"

The app interface was cute. Kind of cartoony. Charlize...*liked* that look, at least sometimes. It wasn't her personal style, but it was okay to look at. Her dad had made fun of the T-shirts she'd worn in high school, with little cats and sheep and fluffy dogs on the chest, and once in a while Charlize could admit she didn't like wearing those shirts so much as she hoped she'd meet someone who liked *seeing* them. The kind of person who'd like a sugar-sweet meme and breakfast in bed first thing in the morning. "You know what, Dad?" she said to the empty office. "I can *like* whatever I *like*." The twinge of spite burned as she filled out a profile.

Once the basics were completed, she circled back to the home screen. *Match of the day.* She had a match of the day! A little sunshine winked saucily and put on a pair of sunglasses.

Okay, *yike*. Curious, though, Charlize tapped the pulsing sunshine anyway. Her match was KyLAUGH. *Is that...Ky-log or Ky-laff?* Laugh, she decided. A text field popped up, and scrolled through suggestions for first lines. She ignored those in favor of "Hello, my match of the day!" And hoped that the match was mutual. Glancing over KyLAUGH's profile, she decided to add another couple of lines. "I see you're in the Boston area. Me too! I didn't realize I could add that to my profile."

She hit send. A colorful wheel appeared, spinning for about fifteen seconds, until another pop-up covered the screen. *Refresh and try again.*

Charlize refreshed as commanded. A check mark appeared next to the message. That was something. Then another pop-up appeared. *Get ready for a match game!* it read. *Find out if you should get together.*

Okay. The screen played a tutorial: She and KyLAUGH would each see a screen with two options, and have a countdown of three to pick between them. *Okay*, again. First up: *Cat or dog?* Charlie button smashed *dog.*

And waited. Then waited some more. She was instructed to *refresh and try again*, so she did. The results appeared. KyLAUGH chose: *cat.*

"I mean, cats are okay too," Charlize said to her phone, like it was listening. "If you'd just let me pick both, I'd have picked both." She had a bad feeling about how this was going to go. The app moved on to the second part of the game. Next up: *Rock, pop, classical, jazz, R&B, or country?*

"Hey, wait, that's more than two!" The spinning wheel of connectivity problems appeared again as she jabbed a finger against the screen, intending to select *rock* but landing on *classical.* Disaster Date informed her that KyLAUGH picked *country.*

A pop-up. *Hmm. You don't seem to have a lot in common yet.*

"Thanks, Disaster Date, I noticed," Charlize said, not even a little embarrassed to be talking back to a phone screen. This app was living up to its name. She was going to leave a review. Or at least a rating.

Last question, and it's an easy one! Hamburgers or pizza?

"Yes," Charlize shouted, choosing *pizza*. A moment later, she remembered that *pizza* was on her profile, so if KyLAUGH picked hamburger, that could mean—

KyLAUGH also chose pizza! the app informed her. *Why don't you two get together over a pie?*

The pop-up closed itself, sending her back to the message chain. There was no response from KyLAUGH. Charlize caught her reflection in the office window. Her V-neck sweater was fitted perfectly. Her hair was messy. And goddamn it, she was *cute*. As cute at this disastrous app. She started typing. "Do you want to come over and have pizza, watch a movie? I'll keep the front door open middle-school style if that makes you feel safe with someone you've never met in person."

Seconds passed. A minute. Charlize put the phone down. It wasn't like she'd set a deadline for a response or suggested a day and time. Or indicated she wouldn't be open to meeting somewhere else. No reason to expect a response yet to an invitation that was open-ended. Open until she deleted this disaster of a situation—

A little typewriter appeared. *Definitely! Tonight?*

"Great! See you at seven?" All adrenaline, Charlize typed in her phone number and address and hit send before stopping to think about how she'd wriggle out of the evening if things went sour. They only had pizza in common.

Yeah!

It was 4:45 p.m.

Charlize bolted out of her chair and started the office closing process. She made sure the coffeepot was empty and washed; she shut down her desktop and packed her messenger bag, then donned her windbreaker and bike helmet.

It was only 4:51 p.m. It was *already* 4:51 p.m. The desk phone rang. "Son of a..." It had to be answered. She unbuckled her helmet and picked up.

A burst pipe in Pine. She noted down the information and turned her computer back on, punching in the number for Maintenance with one hand. A plumber was on the way before she finished inputting the work order. As soon as she'd filled out the incident report follow up reminder, she keyed in the command for the after-hours recording and started her office closing process over. It was a little after 5:30 before she finally locked the office and unlocked her bike.

She zoomed toward home, heart pounding. At the apartment, she rushed to get her things situated and Licorice out for a walk. It was starting to get very windy, and she fumbled with her phone. *Pizza, pizza, pizza.* She needed to get an order in right away if she wanted to have any hope of feeding KyLAUGH at a reasonable hour.

What was she supposed to call her when she showed up? *Ky-log, Ky-laff?* Mikey's Fresh Pizza was estimating forty-five minutes to deliver. She flicked over to Disaster Date, wishing she had KyLAUGH's number so she could text. "What's your pizza topping fave?"

Fortunately, KyLAUGH was on it. "Hawaiian, but I'm up for anything except anchovies and artichokes."

Charlize hated pineapple and loved artichokes, and couldn't legitimately say whether she liked anchovies or not, having never tried them. Licorice tugged at his leash, annoyed that the after-work pace wasn't at his speed, then took a detour to sniff all sides of a tree before deciding which root to pee on. Business over, he rounded the corner toward home and treats. Charlize dragged her feet, putting in an order for one Hawaiian pizza and one tomato-bacon-artichoke. "That's pizza ordered," she said aloud, swiping back to the app to update KyLAUGH.

Licorice heard the magic word, *pizza*, and jumped into her arms, smearing muddy paws across the front of her windbreaker just as Charlize tried to send a message to KyLAUGH about their dinner through Disaster Date. "I know, buddy, I know, I love it too." Her thumb skidded across a series of little images she hadn't seen before, all fall-themed, and she ended up sending, instead of *see you soon*, an icon of a smiling ghost, which glowed, then disappeared.

four

Charlize fumbled with the front door lock. She felt like time was simultaneously not enough and taking forever. The clock was heading toward seven, toward KyLAUGH, but the second hand wasn't moving at all. She hustled Licorice inside and steered him toward the kitchen for water and dinner, then made a frantic dash to sweep a mess of napkins and takeout containers off the coffee table (courtesy Sycamore Hall, five years ago).

She slammed her bedroom door open on the way through to the bathroom to shower. *No. No time.* Wash face, sniff pits, add deodorant just in case, swap sweater for a white t-shirt. There was a little coffee stain on her jeans, where she'd sloshed a few drops over the edge of her mug during a morning meeting, so she peeled them off, hopping to the dresser to retrieve a clean pair, then toppling onto the bed, one ankle caught. "Argh!"

After a few seconds that felt like a few minutes, she was clear, but with a new dilemma. Underwear change? She didn't have even the slightest expectation that KyLAUGH would want to see them, fresh pair or not, but maybe KyLAUGH would expect her to be wearing boxers instead of a thong, based on the rest of her outfit? Elastic up. Elastic down to her knees. Back to her waist. Down.

Stop. When she'd chopped off her ponytail, the responses on dating apps fell off to near zero. Getting a date was a huge boost, and felt really good, but she couldn't let anyone—not her dad, not this new girl—pressure her into being anything except utterly, fully herself.

Her current herself was bare-assed and a little chilly. She dug through her underwear collection: too many B-team pairs, not enough A-team pairs. Expecting particular underwear wasn't fair, but expecting undies without a sneaky hole in them definitely was.

Worst case scenario, she was going to eat some pizza. Better case scenario, she'd make a new friend tonight, too. Ever better scenario, maybe she'd get—

The doorbell rang. Charlize practically jumped into the pair of underwear she was clutching—plaid, granny, dear goodness—and rolled onto her back on the bed to put both legs into her jeans at once. "Coming!" she shouted. *That might be too forward.* "Just a sex! Sec!"

Licorice barked at the front door. Charlize sprinted a lap of the apartment, herded him into the bedroom, and shut the door. "Bed, Licorice. Lie down and take a nap," she called. She hoped that would work until she had a handle on the situation, including whether KyLAUGH liked cats because she liked cats, or liked cats because she disliked dogs.

Charlize snapped open the deadbolt and flung open the front door.

No one was there.

A whoosh of wind blew her back a few steps and knocked her into the wall. How in the world had a storm blown up so quickly, and how had it come all the way inside? *Must have been a freak gust,* she decided.

There were two pizzas on the doormat. Charlize took them to the kitchen and opened them on the countertop. Her tomato-bacon-artichoke was piping hot and delicious-looking, and the other one was Hawaiian. To be fair, it was also piping hot; it simply wasn't going anywhere near her mouth, so she hoped KyLAUGH could take on the whole pie and any leftovers.

She reached out to close the boxes and saw something that terrified her like no unattended candle ever had. One triangle of Hawaiian pizza was wiggling like there was something underneath—a cockroach? A very small rat? She inhaled a deep breath to yell and the piece of Hawaiian lifted into the air, then fell face-down on the linoleum floor.

"WHAT. THE. F—"

A wisp of steam coalesced into the faint outline of a person, and when it faced her way, Charlize could make out a head and shoulders and the faint outline of a mouth, which smiled and silently mouthed, "Hello."

"UCK," Charlize continued.

The ghost moved its mouth again, but still made no sound. It reached for another slice of pizza, which floated upward and lost its steaming toppings before falling to the floor. The figure shrank back into a blob.

Whatever the heck was standing in front of her—maybe a trick of the light, maybe...there was no reasonable explanation for why she was seeing a transparent figure that appeared to be shouting into a void. But whatever it was didn't seem able to hurt anything, so Charlize leaned closer.

She caught a few words when the weirdness moved back quickly before sidling close again. "Hot...like...box...pizza... you..."

"What about the pizza?" Charlize asked softly.

Its shadowy streaks, which Charlize thought were probably arms, disappeared into the crust. The blob tried again, frustrated. It turned her way, waving its arm-ish appendages, and then turned back to the pizza to try again, and this time, the arms went right through the pizza, the box, and the counter.

The visitor let out a scream that Charlize heard in her imagination only, and then it disappeared.

five

She was freaking out.

Where *was* she? *Who* was she?

"Hey, don't—it's okay, it's okay," the red-headed woman was saying. "It's only pizza. It'll wash."

Pizza. She liked pizza. Didn't she? Maybe not. She pushed past the woman, and the...actually really cute woman, reacting slowly, reached out an arm—but didn't catch her.

Beyond the small, dark kitchen was a living room, lit cozily with lamps, and a couch piled with pillows and blankets. A TV sat on a low bookshelf against one wall, and a large mirror hung on the opposite wall, next to another door.

"Did I get hit by a train, or a bus, or something?" she shouted, spinning around in the strange room. "Am I asleep?" She reached for her arm, but there was nothing to pinch. Waving her hand in front of her face, she saw the faintest outline of a palm and five fingers, but it faded when she squinted.

Heart racing, she stepped in front of the mirror and saw—

Nothing.

"Please don't let me be a vampire, please please *please*." She pressed her invisible hand over her invisible stomach and concentrated. There was no desire in her for blood, but she was pretty hungry for pizza. The smell of pineapple and ham permeated the room—her invisible nose worked— competing with a less tasty variation of pizza. So there was a fact: Hawaiian, good; other pizza, bad.

That was one thing she knew. One thing that was real.

The red-haired woman peeked out from the kitchen, but didn't seem to see her. She remembered—she was on her way to see someone. A horse? Something like Charlie's Horse, but she didn't know why. Why would anybody want to have a—

"Charlie Horse," she said, and she felt her tongue move, and air pass through her, and the sound of those words came to her ears. Real.

And the woman heard her this time, and approached, slowly. "Yeah, I'm—you can call me Charlie. I don't know if I like Charli with an *i* or Charlie with an *e*, or Charlize with a *z*, like most people spell my name and what's on my birth certificate, but Charlie's okay. Nobody but my friends ever call me that. You can be my friend and call me Charlie, too." The other woman shoved her hands in her pockets and shrugged her shoulders. She peered around. "Are you still here? Are you...what are you?"

She leaned forward—*flew* forward, without feet, to hug this strange Charlie woman who made friends out of thin air, and *her entire body went right through*. Like her molecules politely moved out of the way, and in that moment when they overlapped, she was colder than she thought a no-body could experience.

It was terrifying.

And not only to her. Charlie let out a yelp. "*Holy hell.* I know it's Halloween, but I refuse to be haunted. I am *not* dying tonight."

Haunted? She let out the loudest scream she could, frustrated and afraid.

Charlie heard that for sure, because she covered her ears and sprang into action, running for the kitchen and slamming open cupboards.

She held her spot in the living room, unsure what to do next. Was the haunting the problem? Or—

A clatter of metal, like a stack of pots falling over, came from the kitchen, and shortly after, so did Charlie. She dumped an armload of supplies on the coffee table. First, she grabbed two shakers—salt *and* pepper—and waved them in all directions, including over her shoulder. "Um, begone!" Charlie shouted. Then she lit a large candle with several wicks.

She sniffed. Apple pie. Mixing with Hawaiian pizza.

From a pile of kitchen gear, Charlie pulled out a small bell and rang it in all four corners of the room before opening the window and turning on a fan that had been tucked behind the couch.

What. "Are you trying to *exorcise* me?" She floated toward the fan and tried to turn it off, but she couldn't find the power switch and her invisible hands wouldn't grasp the cord.

Charlie had her head in her phone. "You have to figure out what you want and what the ghost wants," she muttered.

She spun in a slow circle. "Come *on*. I have a guest coming over soon!"

Great, fine. She planted her feet—the wispy bits that passed for feet—on a navy-and-white rug that she hadn't noticed before. Hard to determine if she liked it or not. "I don't know who I am and I don't know what I want," she shouted at the top of her nonexistent lungs.

To her ears, the words disappeared before they passed her lips, but somehow, Charlie heard her. "You don't know what you want. Sometimes I don't know what I want either." Charlie checked her watch. It was a nice watch, silver and square, on a nice wrist. The fight seemed to go out of Charlie's attitude. "Uh, do you want some pizza? We can try that again."

"YES," she shouted.

Her answer was loud enough. Charlie disappeared into the kitchen again and returned with two plates, one with a slice of gross pizza and one with a slice of pineapple and ham. Skipping the table and chairs that were arranged neatly against the wall separating the kitchen and living room, Charlie brought them to the coffee table, and sat down.

She joined her there on the couch. The Hawaiian pizza smelled better with every passing minute. If she closed her eyes, she could feel the slice and pick it up. She could take phantom bites that filled her up even though the pizza slice hung, whole, in the air above the plate.

"Good, right?" Charlie asked, gnawing on a crust. "Is this what you want?"

"It's better than the delivery by my place," she answered, choosing to ignore that she didn't currently know where her "place" was. And that was true. What memories she had were of undercooked, lukewarm pizza. A box with red type across the top, and a phone number. If she concentrated very, very hard, she could *almost* remember the name of the restaurant.

When she was full, she set the slice of pizza down. "Thanks. That was—you're making me feel almost normal." If she could feel normal again, maybe she could figure out what was going on. Because she was pretty sure that the afterlife, if there was an afterlife, didn't start with pizza and a cute girl who only heard half of what she said and had tried to end her with bell and candle, if not book.

Unless her afterlife *did* start this way. The thought was depressing. She wasn't done with her *life*-life yet. She slid across the couch and rested her head on Charlie's shoulder, squeezing her eyes shut. At least her eyelids still worked.

And her tear ducts.

six

THE PIZZA WAS GETTING COLD and KyLAUGH wasn't coming.

Her spur-of-the-moment date had disappeared in the space of a couple of hours, and Charlie really couldn't blame her. Or—she could, because KyLAUGH could have simply declined, but this sort of thing had happened enough to Charlie over the years that it was hard to blame anybody but herself. Maybe she'd gone a little too hard, jumped from the pickup match to the meetup before everyone was comfortable.

Too much. Too soon.

And the only...person? Thing? Who wanted to hang out was apparently not even real. "Hey, are you still there?" she asked her invisible guest.

Charlie felt a cool draft wrap around her neck, like a chilled scarf—weird—but it was the most comforting cool draft she'd ever felt, and nothing like the earlier deathly chill. If she looked out of the corner of her eye and didn't turn her head too much, she thought she could see someone sitting next to her. A girl. A woman. She had the oddest urge to rub her cheek against the top of the woman's head, to put her arm around this person who was definitely a figment of her imagination.

She always thought about Bayli Dilley around Halloween. Candles in pumpkins reminded her, and old, sad feelings quietly followed her through the last days of October. She'd never talked to anyone about what happened, and her persistent habit of pushing away the things that fucked her was leading up to the grief of finding out, in the form of seeing things that didn't exist.

"I don't know how I died," the ghost said, in a tiny voice hardly louder than a whisper. "Maybe I was crossing the street. I always forget to look both ways, and if there isn't a signal, somebody honks at me and I have to wave like I thought it was my turn and now I'm sorry. But I'm never sorry. I think I should get to go first because I don't pollute the world by walking."

Charlie cheated her chin over to look at the woman resting her forehead on her shirt. She could see her hair, wrapped in a braid around her head. Color: transparent. Her top half had a knit texture like a sweater. If she squinted, Charlie thought she could see the woman's lace-up stompy boots. "Do you know your name?" Charlie swallowed hard. She had to know. "Is it—is it Bayli?"

"No—uh..." The ghost girl hesitated. "Noa?"

"Noa. I like it." Charlie gently leaned forward and slipped her shoulder out from under, then picked up their plates and headed toward the kitchen. The wispy figure followed, watching as she crammed the pizza boxes in the fridge and dropped the dishes in the sink. "Can I get you anything else?" she asked, brushing crumbs from her palms.

Noa leaned over the faucet. "Dishes make me irritable. Don't mind me."

Charlie saw the always-crispy sponge that rested on the edge of the sink lift, then the half-empty bottle of dish soap tilt so blue liquid squirted from its spout. This was so weird. She turned on the tap and Noa scrubbed crumbs and sauce away.

Then, one after another, plates floated from the bottom of the sink—Charlie flinched—and into the draining rack. "There," Noa said, and Charlie was sure she could see a satisfied smile on her oval face. "I always feel better when things are in their places. Clears my head so I can tackle other problems."

Oval face. Braided hair. Sweater. A skirt; corduroy, perhaps. "You don't have to do chores. Really. Come back and sit with me." Charlie held out her hand, and Noa brushed her fingers against her palm. They were cool and soft, and Charlie shivered from the touch, but not because of the temperature. *Dozens of dates and I have chemistry with the ghost.*

She tugged Noa gently back to the couch like Noa was a balloon she didn't want to let go of and watch disappear into the sky. "Let's see what you remember. Are you from around here?"

Noa looked down at her lap and disappeared for a few seconds. Just before Charlie moved to try to find her again, her nose came back into focus, followed by her ears. "I think so. I came on the train. Maybe? Do I know you? Are you from around here?"

"I'm not," Charlie answered. She grabbed her phone and opened the maps app. "Been here since I started college. I still have to look up new places, though. I grew up near Mobile—"

"Oh, I grew up in Kansas!" Noa reappeared fully on the adjacent cushion. "In a house, there were a lot of us...a basketball hoop in the driveway. Enormous yard. But I wanted to live in a big city."

When she knows something for sure... Charlie didn't know how to complete the thought. Was it happy memories? Facts? The act of prompting? "So we both chose Boston and surrounds. Something's keeping me here. And you, too."

The corner of Noa's mouth turned up. Her crooked grin—what Charlie could see of it—was so cute. "I think *you're* keeping me here."

Warmth spread through Charlie, down her neck and across her cheeks. "Uh, heh." She kicked herself mentally. That was a *flirt*. It demanded a witty response. Not that she had one available. "Hopefully not against your will?"

Noa snorted. That seemed to startle her, and she brought a finger to the tip of her nose briefly. "Sorry. I mean, I don't know what my will is right now. Also, did I have a will-will? Did I write one?" She spread her hands on her thighs. Charlie had been wrong before; the skirt was plaid. Or maybe the skirt was shorts. Her features were still unclear, and Charlie didn't want to stare at Noa's nether region for too long.

Gingerly, Charlie took Noa's hand from her lap. Still cool, but substantial. "We'll figure it out. How about an easier question, like your birthday?"

That was a nope, even after a minute's consideration. "I'm a Capricorn," Noa finally offered.

"You were born in the winter. I'm a spring baby. Taurus." Was that one of the signs that was supposed to be a good match for a Capricorn? Charlie couldn't remember. Didn't matter; *ghost* wasn't a match for anyone. *Argh.* She needed to stop her brain from going down that path.

Of course, if you were a ghost, *human* wasn't going to be at the top of your must-have list. Charlie was going to have to live with that. She rubbed her thumb over Noa's knuckles absently. She imagined that she could feel them, the cool, dry furrows where the fingers bent. Funny, really, that after a long, long dry spell, she could feel so connected to someone who wasn't real.

Noa settled back into the couch with Charlie's hand clasped in hers. Charlie's brain filled in a change from cool to warm, to skin as vital as any she had ever touched. "Sorry," Noa said, suddenly. "I think I interrupted something, unless you really like pizza and leftovers."

Charlie's cheeks warmed again to the same temperature that resonated between their palms. "I kinda got ghosted tonight." She regretted the turn of phrase immediately. "I mean, I had plans. My date stood me up. Which is turning out to be pretty awesome, because I got to meet you."

"Good. At least one of us is having a good day." Noa looked at her, eyes glistening, and they laughed at the absurdity of it all.

seven

T_{HEY} _{SAT} _{AT} _{THE} _{TABLE} against the kitchen wall, Charlie straddling a chair turned backward, Noa curled up cross-legged on the other side.

Charlie's stare was intense. Noa held her breath, waiting, until Charlie whispered, low and sultry, sending a shiver up her spine.

"Draw four."

"You bastard," Noa replied.

Charlie arched an eyebrow. "And change to blue."

Maybe she'd draw a blue card to go with her red 9 and yellow 6. She flicked her fingertips along the edge of the deck. "Gosh, can't seem to pick anything up. Guess I'll have to skip that part." The top card slid out of place, and she quickly stacked it back with the rest.

Charlie swept up four cards and, without looking, inserted them into her hand. "Can't let a little incorporeality stop you. I'm starting to think you're not very competitive, Noa."

"Oh, it depends," she said. "I like swimming. No other sports, though. I'll play along, but I don't care about winning." The recollection of chlorine tickled her nose, and she had a dim memory of the sound of a whistle and splashing water, but there wasn't anything concrete to explain why.

Charlie nodded. "I don't really care about winning at sports either. I always liked them, though. Softball, soccer, volleyball, you name it. I couldn't get enough." She rearranged the cards in her hand. "I liked the camaraderie. And the uniforms. I didn't have to look pretty. I only had to show up."

"Did you have to look pretty? When you weren't playing?" Noa considered her options. Blue 7 it was, and the turn passed to Charlie, who was staring at her hand, but focused somewhere beyond her cards.

Maybe that was a little too bold. Charlie didn't seem to hear the last part, at first. "I...I guess so. I always felt like everybody wanted to have a say in how everybody else looked." Charlie ruffled her short hair with one hand, then played another card. "I got over worrying about it. Mostly. Eventually."

Noa nodded. She understood. "*You do you* is the best advice I've ever heard. It should include another part: *You do you and only worry about you.*" She peeled a card out of her stash with a fingernail. The polish on it was chipped. Noa wondered what that meant. Who was the *you* she wanted to be? The you she wanted do at the moment was *Charlie*.

She banished the thought from her brain. Ghosts didn't have sexy thoughts. Or sexy times. "And *I* like you, and I don't want to have a say in how you look. As long as you're happy, I'm happy. I do really like your freckles, though. And your pointy nose. So I hope those make you happy too."

Charlie, card in the air, stalled out. Her generous, enticing mouth opened a little, and closed again. Her cheeks turned a delightful shade of pink. *Flustered.* Noa thought *flustered* was exceptionally attractive. She kept it up as they moved cards from their hands onto the discard pile. *Pink, pink, pink.* "I like your shoulders. I like your t-shirt and your jeans. You look—" She perused Charlie, up and down, letting her gaze linger on everything she could see above the tabletop.

This was a dangerous game.

"You look pretty, and handsome, and pink, and—"

"Uno," Charlie breathed.

"Dammit!" Noa burst into laughter for the second time that night. She had to draw, and Charlie smirked—*sexily*, unfortunately—while she picked up nearly half the remaining deck. House rules. Finally, she had a playable card, which Charlie quickly followed with her last one.

"Noa, Noa, Noa. That was a good trick, but I can't be fooled with sweet nothings."

"I meant what I said," Noa protested. "Can't a girl tell a girl—" The rest of her cards slipped through her fingers and scattered. She felt off—even more off than she did due to her ghostly state. Something about this conversation had happened before.

She'd been questioned. Dismissed.

The details were evading her. And so did her body, flickering and fading. "I'm never going to figure this out," she said, softly. "I don't make any sense."

Charlie gathered up all the cards and tapped the deck on the table, aligning the edges again. Neat. Squared away. Completely unlike her life. Or death. Or whatever this was.

"Don't say that. I think we were getting somewhere." Charlie's smile was fading, and she'd gone pale again, no trace of her earlier blushes. "Besides, who says things have to make sense?"

Noa didn't know. *Someone* said things like that. Before she could argue the point, a phone rang.

Charlie retrieved her phone from her pocket, glanced at the number, and answered. "Hey." She listened, and Noa could hear several excited voices, faintly, through the speaker. They said something about plans, catching a mid-night movie. "Sorry, I'm gonna pass this time. I have company."

This earned Charlie an even louder conversation on the other end, including a squeal Noa suspected only Charlie could translate. Charlie listened and spots of color appeared high on her cheekbones, a hint of her earlier blushes. "Just a friend."

Of course. Crap. It was getting late and Noa was a ghost. A feeling tugged at her, prompting her to run out the door, to disappear. When Charlie hung up, she said, "I should go."

"Go where?" Charlie asked, befuddled. "Noa, you don't remember..." She trailed off, kind enough to not speak the whole truth out loud. "Let's watch some TV and reheat the pizza. See what happens, see if you remember anything." Charlie turned her phone face down on the table, a gesture Noa recognized as silencing any additional calls. "I like having you here."

Just as a friend, Noa's brain supplied. "Okay," her mouth added.

And they curled up together on the couch, Noa wondering if she would have the chance to be part of a team again. Charlie's team, if she had to play the game. And if Charlie was on her team, she'd give everything she had to win.

eight

Charlie hadn't considered that, given the time of year, most of the movies running on regular TV would be horror. Normally, this wouldn't have bothered her; she wasn't much of a horror fan, but that kind of movie was perfect for snuggling on the couch, even the perfect excuse to hold hands—or more. She flicked the button on the remote, past girls making ill-advised jaunts to the basement, a couple of police procedurals, and far too many infomercials. After running through the channel guide a couple times, she landed on an advertisement for toilet paper that usually made her snicker, and turned the remote over in her hands while she tried to come up with a plan, searching her brain for any streaming service passwords, shared with friends, that were currently active. The ad ended, and familiar faces filled the screen—

"This one," Noa said, grabbing her arm and squeezing. "Can we watch this one?"

Charlie was dubious. "As long as you're okay with the concept of being busted. I'm not afraid of no—"

Noa let out a sound like "oop" as she stole the remote and turned up the volume. "I love a woman who knows her shit, okay? And a Faraday cage. Gotta love a Faraday cage."

The news broke in, reporting a problem with the electricity for the T being restored and train service returning to normal following an unexpected failure of power components. Maybe that was why KyLAUGH had bailed without a call or text. Bleh. Charlie slumped back against the cushions. "What's your shit? That is, what's the shit *you* know?"

Noa was quiet for a moment, head tilted. "I know about connecting the dots. I suppose that's my shit." She turned her head and Charlie could see her long lashes. The knit pattern in her sweater, the same cable pattern on a blue sweater from the Gap that Charlie had worn to threads a year ago. If she concentrated, she could almost feel the yarn against her arm, the scraping of the wristband where Noa still clutched her bicep. "I'm having a minor problem connecting them at the moment, that's all. What's your shit, Charlie? What's the thing you know all the way through, backward and forward?"

That was a trick question. How could she answer when she didn't know *so many things*? Charlie knew about change, about her friends. How to walk a dog that didn't want to be walked. Exactly where on her forehead to set her bike helmet. How to make the finicky door at Hickory Hall read her staff card on the first try. How to tell if a couch would fit into a space without measuring. How to rearrange a dorm room based on the looks on new student faces so that they'd stay together instead of requesting a transfer.

"Home," she blurted out. "How to come home. Help people find home." There wasn't a way to translate the knowledge into an explanation that would make sense outside her own head, but Noa seemed satisfied. "I want...home."

"Makes sense." She moved her hand—a hand that had hints of warm gold and sandy beaches—over Charlie's. "I feel at home with you."

The news ended and the movie started again, and they fell silent except for the occasional giggle until the credits rolled. Noa sat up to stretch, and by unspoken agreement, they chair danced until the music cut out and a woman in a stereotypical witch costume came on to tell them the Halloween forecast for tomorrow. "So..." Charlie rubbed the back of her neck. "You'll be staying over, I guess?"

Noa looked around like she had lost all track of time. "Oh, it's late, and I should—"

"Stay here," Charlie cut in. Where was Noa going to go? *Away*, an evil part of her brain insisted. And she wasn't ready for that. Not yet. "I can loan you something comfy to sleep in and I've got extra toothbrushes." She lunged for the door to her bedroom, thinking about long T-shirts and travel-size bath products, and not thinking about Licorice at all.

Licorice wriggled past her as soon as Charlie cracked the door, hackles raised. "Woof!" Licorice proclaimed, followed by a growl and more barking. Ears flat, teeth bared, he rumbled from deep within his chest as Noa tucked her feet underneath herself and—

Hurdled over the coffee table and into the kitchen, Licorice chasing behind. That was where his *food* was, after all, and Charlie stumbled in a circle, not sure if she should go into the bedroom to grab a harness for Licorice or to the kitchen to intervene. It wasn't like Licorice could bite Noa. She wasn't corporeal. "Licorice!"

Licorice needed a stronger command. He chased Noa, who was more visible than Charlie had seen thus far, back into the kitchen. "Licorice, lie down!"

The dog dropped to his stomach, whimpering and growling in turns. Noa dropped to her knees, sobbing and nearly opaque.

"I'm so sorry. I should have—I've never seen him do that." Charlie knelt before Noa, and wrapped her arms around Noa's shoulders. She thought she could smell her, a scent like crisp apples and jasmine, and feel her hot tears on her neck.

"I was scared of dogs when I was little. There was a big black one that would try to bite me when I was walking to the bus stop." She gasped hiccupping breaths that would not be eased by Charlie's gentle rocking. "My mom told me to take a treat in my pocket and eventually we made friends, but until then..."

Charlie rested her chin on Noa's temple, which was surprisingly solid. "That must have been terrifying, especially when you were small." Licorice whuffed where they were pressed together at the hip—Charlie hadn't realized—and she looked down to see Noa's hand under Licorice's chin, scratching softly.

Noa's gaze followed hers, and she saw what she'd been doing unconsciously. A tiny laugh escaped between the tears and hiccups.

"Licorice! I said lie down. Don't be a bad dog." Charlie frowned. "I swear he does know how to behave."

And Noa said, "Good dog." Her lips twisted into a bitter-sweet smile. "He saw me right away. And he thinks I'm real."

They stayed like that, in their little hug huddle on the floor, for a few more minutes until Licorice had had his fill of scritches and left to check on his bowl in the kitchen.

Charlie got to her feet, letting go with reluctance. Noa followed her into the bedroom and accepted her offer of a T-shirt (*Chestnut College, Go Nuts!*) and a pair of shorts, and Charlie fished an extra toothbrush out of her stash. She turned on the light in the bathroom, grateful that she'd swabbed everything down recently, and got out of the way. The sound of water running and a bristle brush assured her Noa was occupied, so she employed her quick-change skills to swap her day clothes for a tank top and boxers. Charlie was getting a blanket down from the closet when Noa reappeared, swimming in the old shirt.

She carefully averted her gaze. "Thermostat's here on the wall, and there are three blankets on the bed, so you should be plenty warm enough, I hope. Wake me if you need anything." Charlie forced her mind not to imagine everything that could be *anything*. "Anything at all."

Noa climbed under the duvet. "You make a cozy bed, Charlie."

Charlie sounded so good coming out of Noa's mouth.

"Well, um, goodnight!" Charlie spun on her heel and made for the living room.

"Charlie? Wait."

She hesitated in the doorway, not daring to turn around. Noa would read her like a book. A picture book. Easy peasy. "Yeah?"

"Hear this with love: Your couch is the most uncomfortable thing my butt has ever touched. I think. Stay in here. There's plenty of room."

Fuck it. Seize the day. Live in the moment. Take nothing for granted. There was a really cute ghost—a really cute *woman*—in her bed. Charlie thought about it. Noa seemed to take this as denial, because she added, "I won't say *oooh, wooo* all night or anything. I'll go right to sleep. Promise."

Licorice came in from the kitchen, tail wagging, and Charlie nabbed his collar as she was pulled into the bedroom, toward Noa.

And Noa was looking at her, duvet pulled up to her chin, glasses off now. Charlie couldn't see them anywhere, and wondered what that meant. She didn't want to think too hard about the details. "Okay," she said. And she promised herself that she'd go right to sleep too.

Easier said than done.

nine

Noa shifted toward the middle of the bed as Charlie came around the side and turned off the light. She hadn't lied about the covers being warm. No harm in being closer to a source of heat, though.

Charlie got into bed gingerly and pulled the duvet up to her chin. "I don't usually take girls to bed on the first date," she said into the darkness.

She could only laugh. "Who says this is a date?" She rolled onto her side and wrapped an arm under her pillow. Close. Maybe a little too close. "Better than the last three I went on, and I nearly got eaten by a dog this time."

The mattress dipped as Charlie rolled her way. "Do you remember something?"

Noa considered. She had a scrap of a memory about being somewhere too loud and too dark. Another half scrap about ordering coffee for two—a memory without an emotion. How long ago did these dates happen? All she was sure of was that there wasn't anyone waiting for her at home, wherever *home* was. "I don't usually take girls to bed on the first date either."

A line of light limned the doorway—a lamp was still on in the living room—but it wasn't bright enough to see Charlie's expression. Charlie's long exhalation and *hmm* told Noa that she was smiling, probably.

"What kind of dates do you go on?" Charlie asked her, yawning.

Noa had to match the yawn. That wasn't fair. She tried to describe the two she could remember—her assertion of three bad dates was a lie. "Clubbing, recently. It was too noisy for anything but dancing and I..." She took a moment to figure out what to say, to figure out what had happened. There was so little memory there. "I didn't know my date very well, and I wanted to talk first. Another time, it was coffee. But coffee feels like too much talking and not like dating."

Charlie really did laugh at that. "I can see it. I love coffee, though. I even drink it"—she let out another splitting yawn—"on my days off. Usually before I feel like talking. That comes later."

She snuggled closer to the middle of the bed. They were almost touching. Noa could feel the warmth radiating off Charlie, feel Charlie's exhalations ruffle the loose strands of hair at her temples. "Charlie?"

"Yeah?"

"Those dates." Noa wasn't entirely sure about *all* of her dates. Only the last few. And she wanted to be clear instead of joking. "I went on dates with girls."

"I do that too," Charlie whispered. "Go out with girls."

A rush of excitement started in Noa's toes and sprinted up her skin, tingling her scalp. Parts of her that she hadn't been able to feel a few hours ago were reminding her that they existed, that they could feel too. She remembered herself. What she wanted. "What are those first dates like, the ones where you don't take those girls to bed?"

Charlie shifted. Her arm slid against Noa's—*god*, she had skin again. Felt where her skin was again. The first rush of sensation eased into relaxation. Her eyelids were heavy.

"Well, pizza and a movie is a decent first date. I mean, we had a pretty good time, right?"

Noa felt her head droop forward, onto Charlie's shoulder, where she'd gone for comfort all evening. Charlie was safe where nothing else was.

"Museums are good."

Noa nodded. She liked museums. Didn't she? Art museums.

"Maybe a ballgame."

Ballgame. Games. There was something she should know about those.

"Whatever I can convince somebody to do, even if we've only ever messaged on some dating app."

"App," Noa repeated. *App.* She was supposed to know something about apps. Or *an* app. Maybe she'd met someone on an app. The thought was slipping away as fast as sleep was coming for her.

The bed dipped with a sudden, bounding weight. "Licorice, get down," Charlie said.

"S'okay," Noa said, voice muddled by sleepiness. Licorice nosed for a spot between them, tags jangling, but there was no room. "Ghost is taking up his spot. My bad."

Charlie bent her legs as Licorice circled, and she and Noa tangled together beneath the sheets. Noa felt her ankle against Charlie's ankle, her knee against Charlie's knee. There was something she was supposed to remember. Something about dogs. Dogs and cats and apps and dates.

But the bed was so good. Charlie was so good.

Tomorrow. She could remember tomorrow. And now it was dark and her body was soft and her eyes were closed.

She felt a soft brush of fingertips against her cheek. Charlie said, "Licorice has his own spot, and I don't mind you taking up this one."

And then she was gone.

ten

In the morning, the first thing she heard was "You're still here." The curtains were open, and watery autumn sunlight lit Charlie from behind, tracing her outline in gold. Noa reached for her.

Her hand was invisible again.

Noa craned her neck to see herself. The duvet was puffed up in a giant lump, but there was nothing else to see. "I'm still here," she said, to prove it to herself, if not to Charlie. Her mouth was frowning—that she could feel—but why did she have to start over? She wanted to be whole again. She wanted to know—

Charlie didn't seem to notice that she was fading. "I think we should go out," Charlie said, stretching her arms over her head.

She sat up, and the duvet folded away. Though her long-term memories were still a murky haze, her short-term memory was fine. She remembered threading her limbs through Charlie's, remembered their admissions that their preferred partners were in the realm of: each other. "Go out...on a date?"

That earned her a grin. A wide, lopsided grin that was as bright as the sun streaming down on the bed. "I was thinking go out and see if we can discover who you are and how you got here. Get you home."

Noa flopped back down on the mattress, hoping her invisibility hid her disappointment. Her partial disappointment. She *did* want answers. And Charlie was on the right track. She was simply avoiding the questions in case they led her somewhere terrible.

Charlie disappeared into the bathroom for a shower, and Noa filled the time snooping around the apartment. It was her right, as a ghost, to open the closet and brush her fingers against the other woman's sweatshirts and jeans, to investigate the spines of a dozen books that shared a side table with a soccer ball and a tennis racket. There was a vintage Jurassic Park poster taped to the wall next to a framed photo collage of Charlie at different ages: little and playing T-ball, bigger and crossing her arms defiantly over a tutu, taller and stretched up to block a spiked volleyball. Farther on, Charlie's kitchen cupboards were cramped but not crowded; she owned only a few pots and pans, and the pantry was mostly cereal and instant ramen.

To make herself useful, Noa found bread and popped two slices into a toaster that had to be older than Charlie herself. She pushed the knob down with difficulty. Her arms were kind of tired today. It was surprisingly draining to not be able to see her own hand in front of her face. And the half-empty jar of peanut butter was heavier than she expected, but she eventually managed to scrape a thin layer of it over both pieces of toast and scrub the knife in the sink before sliding to the linoleum floor with her breakfast. Licorice came up beside her, tail wagging. He sat down, sniffing his interest in her toast without any visible alarm that a piece of bread was floating in the air. Noa realized she could see the frames of her glasses in her peripheral vision again. Charlie appeared next, hair damp and cheeks pink from the shower. "Licorice, no begging."

"It's okay," Noa said, tearing off a corner of her toast and slipping it to him. "I feel seen. Also, I don't think I'm allergic to peanuts, which I don't know if I would have remembered." She angled her chin upward. "There's a piece on the counter for you."

"Thanks." Charlie turned away. "I see that you're dressed, so I'll take it with me while I take Licorice for a quick walk before we go," she said, from somewhere beyond the kitchen. The front door opened and closed.

Noa looked sidelong at herself. She could see her green sweater had three ivory stripes across the chest, and she had on a brown corduroy skirt, and tights, and boots. And she could feel a beanie holding down her braid, and she had a book-sized cross-body bag hung over her shoulder. She ran a hand over it—there was a phone inside for sure—but when she tried to unsnap its flap, her fingers melted away.

After a while, Charlie came back in a hoodie and running shoes, with a baseball hat for extra warmth. "Ready?"

She was far, far from ready. But she was going anyway. Noa raised her hand, and Charlie pulled her up and toward the door.

"Wait," she said, turning back one last time. For a temporary home, Charlie's place wasn't so bad, and she wanted to remember it since she couldn't remember any-thing else. Licorice poked his nose outside, but sat obe-diently when Charlie ordered him to stay.

Noa leaned in for one last pet, and whispered, "Thanks for always treating me like a person." Then she cocked her head to one side, and said in a different voice, "Sorry about the barking and chasing, pretty lady, can't believe it all ended in peanut butter only a day later."

"What?" Charlie waited, keys in hand, ready to lock up.

"Nothing," Noa answered, and headed outside. "Just making sure he got to say goodbye."

☾

Charlie wolfed down her toast on the way to the train and was done before she found a seat on the green line headed east. It wasn't busy, so she and Noa sat together, Charlie leaning against the end of a row of seats. "I've always liked this train," Noa said. A confused expression crossed her face. "I guess. I mean, I would like this train if I'd always liked it?"

"It'll get you where you need to go," Charlie said softly, searching her features for answers. Dappled sun leeched the color from Noa's entire being—or Charlie hoped it was only the sun. To lose Noa now— "And I like living in this neigh-borhood. Close to work, good people. Have you remem-bered where you live?"

Noa shook her head in denial. "I do sort of remember an apartment I used to live in. There was a hallway, and I had to pass the other bedroom and a bathroom to get to my room. The hallway light was out and I didn't like that." She shivered. "That's all I remember."

"You had a roommate!" Charlie whispered, sitting straighter in her seat. "Maybe somebody's looking for you right now. If we search missing persons—"

"No." Noa clutched the strap of her purse across her chest like it was a shield. "I don't have a roommate anymore."

Strange how she could be so sure of that and not be able to explain where she lived, Charlie thought, but then Charlie had no idea what it was like to be a ghost. All she knew was that with each block the train passed, the outline of Noa got weaker, and all that stood between Noa's complete disappearance was the hushed conversation that at least one passenger across the aisle was trying to politely ignore.

"Me neither." Charlie pulled the neck of her hoodie away from her shoulders. The gradual increase in the train's passengers had heated the interior to a level that slicked steam over the windows. "I keep thinking I should move in with one of my friends, and then thinking that I might start seeing someone and that could be awkward. You can move too fast and end up in the wrong place." She used the back of her hand to rub a clear circle in the middle of the nearest window. "And now I'm a little older and wiser, and I wonder if I moved too slow."

Noa searched her face, leaving Charlie feeling naked as a baby. How was it that ghosts could look through you when, obviously, *they* were the transparent ones?

The train eased into a station and a crowd boarded, rushing for the remaining seats. An older man hitched up his pants while eying the seat next to Charlie, and she remembered again that Noa was invisible to everyone else. Just before the man's butt hit the bench, Noa catapulted herself into Charlie's lap. "This seat taken?" she asked, mouth against Charlie's ear.

Charlie squeezed her eyes shut and balled her hands into fists against her thighs, trying not to laugh (and trying not to touch her new seatmate). Then she leaned back just enough to see Noa, who smirked wildly. There was no way to answer her now, not with the older man sniffing back a wad of snot and craning over them to look outside.

Noa raised her feet and put her boots in the main's lap. He didn't react, and she sighed and wriggled on Charlie's legs, clearly uncomfortable. Charlie could feel her every outline. Noa's bottom on her thighs. The curve of Noa's chest against her sweatshirt, the tickle of yarn where Noa's arm tangled under her hood. Charlie propped an elbow on the windowsill and tried not to look like she had an entire invisible human in her lap. An invisible human who smelled like jasmine and made Charlie's cheeks warm and her back ache to arch.

She was going to hell.

Or jail, if she forgot herself and anyone looked too closely. Charlie fixed her gaze on the ceiling while Noa twisted to look out the window. "Here," she said, and stood abruptly. Noa walked through the crowded car as if it were empty.

"Wait," Charlie managed, shouldering through the crowd that ignored her repeated requests to "excuse me." She stuck her arm through the door before it closed. It ricocheted off her wrist and she was outside, chasing a ghost across the street.

Charlie followed Noa into the Boston Public Garden. The grounds were showing off, trees colorful. She'd have liked to linger a moment, maybe take a few pictures, but Noa was disappearing ahead. Charlie rushed to catch up. "What's the deal? Did you remember something?"

"Last summer," Noa said, not slowing down even a little. "Date. Here. There was a truck. We got ice cream and walked around, looking for somewhere to sit. My cone melted on the back of my hand, and the back of my neck got sunburned. I had sprinkles." She stopped walking at a statue of George Washington and squinted up at him.

"That's good!" Charlie took a second to catch her breath, hands on her head. "So maybe if you remember who your date was, I could find them and say I'm looking for you. Maybe they'll know something, like where you live, or your name."

"My date thought that Washington fought in the Civil War. For the Confederacy. And thought that was great." Noa was moving again, heading east onto the mall. She fiddled with the zipper on her purse, but didn't open it. "I blocked them. I don't remember anything else."

Charlie dashed after Noa until she could slot her hand under Noa's palm. Not demanding, not grabbing, merely offering hers to hold. Noa looked down, as if she were surprised to see her arm—her arm that Charlie could see, her arm that Charlie was unsure existed for anyone else in the world—and twisted her fingers through Charlie's. They were hot and sweaty. Like real fingers.

God, this was confusing.

The mall was draped in even more autumnal glory than the park. Charlie held Noa's hand, and breathed, and walked with her, counting steps until Noa was less agitated and she said, "It was a bad date, and I remember that I decided I wasn't going to have any more bad dates. I had this important idea...." She frowned. "I can remember the *why*, not the what." Noa squeezed Charlie's hand and swung it, just a little. Like Charlie would have swung Noa's in happiness. "All of this is familiar. A little."

"Then let's keep going," Charlie urged her. A golden leaf fell and caught on the sleeve of Noa's sweater, then gently fluttered to the ground. Almost real. Noa started at the leaf that and then let Charlie pull her along. "Gotta get you home before the witching hour."

Wherever home was, Charlie was going to help her find it.

She always took care of her ghosts.

eleven

NOA LOVED THE PARK, THE mall, the waterfront. She loved them like old friends, not like a girl on a first date seeing them for the very first time. But she wasn't quite *home*.

And even if she could find home, would she be able to open the door? There was the big dramatic question: *Can you ever go home again?* Asking it made her feel stretched thin in all directions. Her hand disappeared again and she stuffed the feeling into her pocket, only briefly pleased to discover her skirt had two of them. She looked around as they came to the end of the mall and crossed over to a sidewalk that skirted stately, well-kept residences.

"Anything look right around here?" Charlie asked.

It was getting harder to remember even as things started to feel familiar. She liked the red brick and bow-windowed sitting room of a four-story house on a friendly corner. But that didn't mean it was *hers*. Maybe nothing was hers. Maybe this was all she was going to have.

Maybe she would be lost soon.

She looked down. Her purse was still there. Her sweater wasn't.

If she had to go out of this world for good, this wasn't the worst way, holding hands with a cute woman on a crisp fall afternoon, with the smell of wood smoke in the air and the sun in her eyes. She closed them, letting Charlie navigate cracks in the sidewalk and street crossings for them, until they stopped at a bench under a tree thick with red leaves. "Let's take a load off."

Noa sat down. The sun was low, and the bench was shaded and cold. When Charlie laid an arm across the back slats, Noa gratefully ducked underneath. She should have brought a jacket. She didn't *have* a jacket. Not here, anyway. She closed her eyes again, willing away whatever destiny was creeping toward her.

That didn't last. A line of children and parents trickled around a corner and onto the end of the mall. There were glittering fairies and rotting zombies, dogs in plush pumpkin coats, witches and basketball players, and even—

A *ghost*. Its costume was gauzy and light, trailing in the breeze. Noa stepped into the line of the parade, touching it gently on the arm. It shrieked and giggled, and then grabbed its mother's hand. The next child, a cockeyed Frankenstein, jumped, then shouted, "I love Halloween!" A dachshund sniffed her feet, and she hop-skipped over it before it could follow her and tangle its leash around a pajama-clad dragon, who felt Noa's touch and let out a giant roar. Her little sisters, both dressed as dragon eggs, screamed in delight.

Noa's contribution to the parade was noise, and she felt alive, so alive.

But not opaque. Charlie was looking past her, and that scared her more than any haunted hayride. Hayride. When had she been scared of hay? Why would she be scared of hay? Nothing more came to mind. She sat back down next to Charlie.

"I don't suppose you remember any costumes you've worn on any past Halloweens, of the sort you'd have posted to social media."

Charlie was so hopeful, she hated to disappoint her. "Not really," she replied, truthfully. "Tell me about yours instead."

"Mostly, I did that." She lifted her chin toward the tiny ghost, who was screeching *woooooo* and running in circles, chased by their parents. "I was always pressured to dress up, and it always seemed like my options were a lot of makeup and frills or sexy animals or whatever the trend was that year, and it was always a tiny-ass costume. An old sheet was the perfect way out."

"Why?" Noa tilted her head. Charlie's face was sad. She didn't know why; Charlie wasn't frowning, or crying, but she was sad nonetheless. "Costumes are just outsides."

Charlie flipped her Red Sox cap backward and leaned forward, elbows on her knees. "Clothes are just outsides."

"Clothes too," Noa agreed. "All our clothes are just outsides. Charlie, are you worried about that?"

Charlie shoved her face into her hands. "I— sometimes."

"I see you," Noa whispered. "No matter what outsides." She heard a sniff and wrapped her arms around Charlie, squeezing as hard as she could. "Charlie—"

"It's okay," Charlie said, sitting up and pressing Noa's hands against her chest. "I didn't realize until now, but I needed to hear that." She shot Noa a watery smile and laughed. "As long as I'm the one who gets to pick the costume I wear."

"Always." Noa touched Charlie's cheek. "Breathe with me," she said. In four, hold four, out four, hold four. She couldn't feel the single streak left behind by the tear that left a stain there. But still she watched, and waited, as the worried lines in Charlie's forehead eased, and as her shoulders morphed from hard stone to softness.

A change.

The kiddie costume parade coalesced into a moving entity again, and Noa watched them disappear. Just like her, disappearing. "Speaking of outsides, my outsides are getting hard to see. Charlie, I think—I think I might have to go soon." All she could do was hold onto her insides. Her insides that were ambitious, that had plans, that were learning to code. "I was learning to code!"

She stood up and started walking as fast as her legs would carry her, toward Fenway Park. She was making an app. There were still things left to do, if only her outsides would come back to her.

Charlie came with her. The sun was sinking. She had to hurry. The people wandering past bars and shopping and getting in her way were so irritating. And where had all these annoying kids come from? She had to get home, home before—

Her feet took her along a quieter side street, and she stopped outside a well-kept modern building. This surprised her a little. Where was the charm, like Charlie's apartment had? This place was sleek, industrial. Safe, though, she decided.

"Is this it?" Charlie reached a hand in her direction, but apparently thought better of it. *All for the best.* She was almost gone. Time was up.

"What if I can't get in?"

"Let me walk you home," Charlie said. "Then we'll see. We'll see as we go."

"Just, see?" she asked.
"It's the least I can do. I mean, you—you see me for me. Let me see what I can see for you."

Noa wanted to press herself into Charlie's chest, cover her face, block out the world. Be in her arms, where nothing ever ended. The seconds ticked by. She patted her purse. There was no key inside. "Maybe I can walk through the door."

Charlie went first, up the black metal stairs, to a landing with three heavy doors. "Here, or farther up?"

Noa cleared her mind, hoping her body would remember. Her toes were pointed a tiny bit to the left, at a red metal door with a keypad on it. That guess was as good as any. "This one."

Charlie turned on her phone's flashlight. There was no illumination outside. Noa remembered that there was supposed to be a porch light on a timer. The building mana-ger reset it once a month so that the light would turn on precisely at sunset. Tomorrow, day of the dead, there would be light at this time of day.

"Are you sure?"

It was so, so hard to think. "The code is six six zero, six six six."

"Oh wow, that's terrible." Charlie punched in the number and the door lock clicked. No fool, she slipped her hand into her sleeve and pressed down on the handle, open-ing it an inch. "What, just in case."

Noa didn't disagree. If she'd had strength in her arms, she'd have done it herself. No fingerprints to leave behind. There were no lamps burning inside the apartment, no alarms blaring a break-in, no nosy neighbors peeking out their doors to see what the commotion was all about. "Okay, I'm going in."

"Wait!" She had to do it herself. "What if...what if I'm in there?"

Charlie raised a hand, like she wanted to press her palm to Noa's cheek, then pressed it against her own. "Then we'll figure out what's next. Together."

Noa clasped Charlie's wrist. "Say goodbye to me here." She raised herself on her toes and brushed her lips across the back of Charlie's hand where it touched her cheek. Charlie turned her head toward the kiss, and Noa knew— she couldn't do that again.

She had to let go.

But there was no goodbye. Charlie simply disappeared.

twelve

NOA'S APARTMENT WAS DREADFULLY DARK. The curtains were closed: blackout.

Charlie flicked her phone's flashlight forward, making her way through the living room. She saw a comfy white couch covered in pillows, and noticed a glass coffee table right as her knee clunked into it. "Ow," she whispered, and then felt dumb for whispering.

Still.

The kitchen was empty. Not even dishes in the sink. Yeah, that was like Noa. Not that she *knew* Noa. But she knew enough. Charlie edged around a corner and nudged open a door that turned out to be the bathroom. She whipped open the shower curtain. Clean white tiles. A bottle of shampoo. A loofah. A couple of razors. Nothing that would prove or disprove Noa's residency.

That left the bedroom. If she was going to find a body, this was going to be where it all went down. Charlie wasn't the church-going type, or even Catholic, but she made the sign of the cross in the air. There were probably other charms to use. She couldn't think of any at the moment, unfortunately. "Here we go, Red Sox, here we go," she chanted under her breath. As good a prayer as any.

Charlie wrapped her hand in her sweatshirt again and turned the knob.

She stood there, waiting for someone to scream, or for an alarm to go off, or—

And she pushed the door so it swung open to reveal a room.

One bed. Made. Too many pillows, *again*, one fuzzy and pink. A dresser, white, probably from IKEA. She flicked her phone that way and illuminated the socket head screws. *Yep, IKEA*. She'd built or dismantled most of the IKEA catalog over the years, and figured the dresser, only available for the past few seasons, meant the owner of the apartment was roughly her age, maybe a little younger.

Could be Noa's. If Noa had died recently.

No. She wouldn't think about that.

An open closet revealed skirts and slacks hanging neatly above a laundry hamper that spilled dirty clothes out onto the floor, where a striped rug was positioned under the bed. She walked around both sides and peeked underneath. The old school digital alarm clock blinked over to 6:23, and Charlie exhaled. For good measure, she exhaled for four.

No bodies. Not even any ghosts.

She turned to rush back out to Noa, and when she did, her flashlight drifted past a desk setup she'd seen, dimly, on her way in. Big. Two monitors. There were papers and notebooks stacked messily on top. Charlie wrapped her hand back in her sleeve. Maybe there'd be a bill or a postcard that would reveal—

There, on the wall above the desk, was a set of carved letters hanging on wires. They were each painted differently, and the cutesy design didn't match the rest of the décor, so Charlie knew they were special. They read:

KYLA.

Ky—

Laugh.

A breeze raised the hair on the back of her neck. Noa was at her elbow.

"This is me," Noa said, softly. "Sorry I ghosted you."

A sound that was half a laugh and half a moan escaped Charlie's mouth. "Every time. Every single damn time."

Noa—*Kyla*—sat down on the couch, her limned form fading into the shadows. "Please leave now."

"Kyla…"

"Please." She was quiet for so long Charlie thought she could never speak again. "I'm home and I'm not alive. I can't be here. Not with you. Not like this." Her face was hidden in the darkness. "It's the only thing I ask of you."

Charlie left. She didn't remember closing the front door or winding back through the streets to the T stop. The train approached, and the lights were blinding. That was what made her eyes water. Not the awful despair of losing the best thing that had happened since she adopted Licorice.

She stuffed her hands in her pockets, gripping her phone. Thinking. About getting the suggested match on that sketchy little dating app. Feeling her heart leap with possibility, because a first date is all about possibility.

The doors opened and she managed to step to the side to let the passengers off. And after the match, only a day ago, she'd biked home, feeling foolish for pedaling and texting at the same time, but also feeling excited for the first time in forever. She was much less excited to be on the train.

Lingering by the doorway, she looked for a seat, but everything was taken by grownups on their way to parties or home from jobs, and little pirates and witches and monsters. And a cute ghost, like the one her thumb brushed during that exchange she'd had with Kyla on the app when—

Shit.

Shit.

Shit shit shit shit.

She shoved an arm into the closing doors and forced her way back out onto the platform. Where—back the way she came. She hadn't paid attention to the streets, and found herself jogging around the blocks, over and over, her chest tightening with every step until she finally saw the dark door to Kyla's apartment. Charlie stumbled up the steps, her hand swollen with exercise and the growing cold when she fisted it to knock.

No answer.

Charlie closed her eyes and rubbed her palm over her face. God, this was—this was unbelievable. She was one hundred percent outside reality.

So that would be her defense when the police asked why she was breaking and entering. Was it breaking and entering if you had the keycode? She couldn't remember. *Six six zero, six six six.*

She didn't see Kyla, but the living room was cold, and blue shadows crawled in the corners. *This place is haunted.* And she'd have to hope it was haunted by Kyla herself.

"Kyla, you didn't ghost me." Charlie wanted so very badly to see her, to not have to say out loud the truth she suspected. "I think I...kinda ghosted *you*. We were talking about dinner and something weird happened." Her cell was stuck in her pocket, but eventually, she retrieved it. The battery meter icon was at 2%. *"God dammit."* Then 1%. Then nothing.

No way around it. She was going to have to go balls to the wall, fingerprints to the...everywhere, she guessed. Charlie thought there had been a charging cord plugged into a power strip on the desk. She groped, tipping over an empty Dunkin' cup and knocking a candle off the edge. *Cinnamon.* She patted her way from one end of the desk to the other, fingers still numb, until she grasped a cord. "Sorry. Nothing's broken. I didn't mean to touch anything anyway. Not now, without asking. I also mean before, in the app we were chatting on."

Stop. Think. Don't babble. Charlie felt her way to the end of the cord. She couldn't tell if it was the right kind of connector. Its end finally slid into the port of her phone— relief—and the startup sequence initiated. That didn't take long, but as soon as she tapped her PIN, it auto-ran an up-date, filling the screen.

Charlie sank onto the floor, sucking in gasps of freezing air. She should have shut the door. All the warmth had left the room and any minute, someone would notice she was where she wasn't supposed to be and she would be in so, so much trouble. If she didn't die of hypothermia first. "Kyla, come back. I—I really want to play Uno with you again and have you stay over so we can talk all night." She clutched the charging phone like a lifeline. The tiny amount of heat that radiated from the case wasn't enough. Icy fingers reached into her and grasped her heart. "You see that my outside is my outside and my inside is me. And I don't care if your out-side and your inside are transparent. I...I like you. And I think you like me. You feel like home."

A soft *ding* announced the end of the phone update and Charlie scrambled for the app. This was so ridiculous. She was ridiculous.

Open app.

Messages.

Profile. Ky-LAUGH. Beneath her photo was a grayed-out icon of a ghost. Deep breath. Charlie tapped it.

The rushing wind that filled the room was almost unbearable. Papers went flying, her hat was lost, the Dunkin' cup clonked Charlie on the knee, and the windows flew open like the world was ending. Lightning crashed and a storm blew inside. She struggled to her feet, breathing brimstone and smoke, nearly tripping over a carved pumpkin that rolled past, its candle snuffing out as she jumped aside. "What is that?"

"Charlie."

She looked into the maelstrom and there was a voice, a face—she stretched out a hand, pulled Kyla into her arms, pressed them together with everything she had—

And the wind turned into a breeze, and a fan, and nothing, and they were standing together in a pile of leaves up to their ankles in the middle of Kyla's living room. Kyla's crown of braids was loose and full of stems. "Hi, Charlie," she said, and it was the sweetest sound ever.

"Are you here with me?" Charlie asked, no longer sure what, if anything, was real, but hopeful that Kyla's smile, and Kyla's arms, and Kyla's mouth, were.

Kyla grinned. "Yeah, I'm here. And I think I'm done with dating apps."

"Me too," Charlie said. "I...I was hoping you, uh, might be up for pizza sometime."

Kyla's arms were tight around her waist. "Now?"

"Now, if you're hungry." Charlie wrapped her arms around Kyla's waist, a mirror image. She was real, and true, and she smelled like jasmine. Charlie leaned back and grabbed her phone, careful to keep it on the charger as she swiped it open.

"I *have* been a ghost all weekend." Kyla tilted her face up to Charlie's. "So I could eat. Let's get Hawaiian *and* your artichoke thing," she said, watching while Charlie put in their order. Her lips were so close, and Charlie knew exactly what she wanted when she said, "And I have a special toppings request."

Which was why Charlie leaned forward and kissed her.

thirteen

Charlie kissed her and she came alive.

Every cell, every molecule, every connection and chip and circuit buzzed with the electricity of Charlie's lips on hers. Kyla wanted to never be *un*alive again, because she never wanted to stop feeling this way. "I made the app," she said, wishing her mouth would *just shut u*p.

Charlie pulled back and looked at her, puzzled. "You—it was yours? Why did your app..." She trailed off, and Kyla didn't blame her.

"I am going to take it down tonight and I think I will go back to school before I make the jump to building my tech empire. And I'm going to write all the code myself, without any assists from AI, next time." Kyla reached an arm over Charlie's shoulder and brushed her thumb against the soft bristle at the nape of her neck. Charlie couldn't hide the look of concentration that crossed her face with each swipe. "Know anywhere with a weekend grad program?"

"As it happens," Charlie answered, pausing to roll her head back into Kyla's touch, just a little, "I know a place. Not too far from me. I could show you around. Show you." Her speech disappeared into a soft noise of approval.

Kyla nodded. "Show me."

Charlie took Kyla's hand from behind her head and led her over the pile of leaves and into her bedroom, which was relatively unaffected by the windstorm, only a few leaves scattered at the entry. There, Kyla switched off the lead and took Charlie toward the bed, pulling her down onto the duvet, where they lay face to face, knees touching, hands entwined. Charlie kissed her in strange places—the outer tip of an eyebrow, her third knuckle, the spot just to the left of her nose. And it still felt amazing. What about today *hadn't* been weird?

Weird was good.

She kissed Charlie back in weird places. The little mole between her lips and her jaw. The place at her temple where her hair was mussed. The tip of her pinky to the back of her hand. And then her mouth, not weird, all warm and soft. Her tongue licked Charlie's top lip; her teeth bit the lower one, drawing forth a groan.

Groan was good.

She wanted more. Kyla pushed Charlie's sweatshirt up, then hesitated. "This okay?"

Charlie sat halfway up and wriggled out of her hoodie, then kicked her shoes onto the floor. "Sorry about the shoes on the bed—"

Kyla sat up and cut her off with a kiss, and Charlie took them back down, an arm beneath Kyla, the other cradling her face. Charlie *saw* her. Saw her as someone to touch. To hold.

Their kisses edged deeper, and Kyla's hand—the one not clutching the front of Charlie's shirt for dear life—trailed over everything she wanted. Charlie's cheekbones, her neck, her hip, where she clung tightly, fingers winding into the pocket of Charlie's jeans.

Charlie felt it too. Their breaths became gasps, their gasps turned to desperation. Kyla tugged and Charlie rolled on top of her, pressing down, one leg between hers, and she instinctively arched upward into the feeling, connecting, *living.*

The doorbell rang.

The tension in Charlie became a sigh, and she buried her face in Kyla's shoulder before rolling off. "Next time I'm ordering from somewhere a little farther away."

Yeah. Kyla smiled up at the ceiling. "Next time." Hopefully a lot of next times.

And they went into the living room and sat on the couch, toasted their slices of pizza together like they were glasses of the finest champagne, and Kyla kissed Charlie on the cheek. "Hey, boo."

Charlie groped on the floor for the pumpkin that was still hiding under dead leaves. Kyla appreciated the way she set it neatly on the coffee table. One thing, already righted. "So...match of the day? What do you think about seeing each other more often?"

Kyla groaned, and laughed, and they put their heads together, close. "You know, you should give Disaster Date five stars. It's been a whirlwind."

"And you saw right through my mask," Charlie said, chewing on a crust. "I hate to eat and run, but I need to go home for a bit."

Obviously. Kyla thought a moment, and suggested, "What if we swing by and take Licorice out for a tour of the neighborhood? Practice. Can't bark at every ghost you see."

"As long as this activity comes with *spirited* discussion," Charlie offered, and kissed her one more time. They put the pizza boxes in the fridge, and Kyla locked the door, and as they walked into the chilly autumn air, arm in arm, she would have sworn that the jack-o-lanterns on the doorsteps were winking at them.

What the hell. She winked back. No more tricks. She was real again. Everything was going to be treats from here on out. *Happy Halloween to us.*

about the author

Waverly Decker is a writer, editor, and (most importantly) reader of books of all kinds. *The 30-Day Engagement*, about two women who fake a relationship so that one can succeed in business—and also show her ex-fiancée that she has finally moved on after being unceremoniously dumped—is her debut novel. She is also the author of a novella: *Girl Gets Ghosted*. She lives in New York.

You can visit her online and sign up for her newsletter with book alerts and promotions at waverlydecker.com.

Read on for two chapters from *The 30-Day Engagement*!

Emory needs a win, a promotion...and a date to her ex-fiancée's Hollywood wedding in this sapphic fake-relationship rom com.

Emory Jordan has been rising through the ranks of the boys' club at a venture capital firm in New York, where she's competing for her dream promotion. When Emory's estranged ex-girlfriend Mari—who broke off their engagement to pursue her acting ambitions—sends her a wedding invitation, it's the perfect opening for Emory to pitch a business deal to Mari's new tech mogul fiancé. More importantly, it's a chance for Emory to prove to Mari that she has moved on from their breakup. The wrench in her plans: she's been putting work at the top of her to-do list, and there's nobody she can ask to be her plus-one.

But Emory has a knack for business strategy. Bliss Tully, who's a struggling florist with a good-vibes-only attitude, accidentally stabs her with a cactus, and Emory sees an *opportunity*. Bliss is short on trust—her father's white-collar crimes left her with a deep aversion to the business world—but she's also short on cash, so she agrees to pose as Emory's fiancée. The job is only for a month and pretending should be easy money. Right? Mari's wedding approaches, and Emory and Bliss grow closer, all too aware their engagement is nothing more than a thirty-day sham. As far as kissing the bogus bride, though, they both want to say *I do*....

You are cordially invited to the fakeout in this slow-burn contemporary lesbian romance about letting go of the past—and loving your future.

one

EVERY SUMMER, WW AND PARTNERS held a lunch with all the interns. These interns, alternately awkward or overconfident, with a few partners and VPs, shuffled into the wood-paneled conference room for a sandwich and a seltzer water, and sat together at the long, polished table in the company's largest meeting room, which technically overlooked Bryant Park but actually faced the upper floors of a dozen other charmless midtown Manhattan office buildings. A few platitudes were shared, a few handshakes exchanged, and then everyone went back to work, the interns to be mentored by the most junior analysts in the most isolated cubicles, far from the real action.

But one phrase from that lunch had stayed with Emory Jordan since she was hired as an intern twelve years ago. She'd carried it with her as one of the few women to work at WW and Partners—through her years as an analyst, while climbing her way through the associate ranks, and into her years as a VP. The advice had come from the current WW himself, William Wils. William was the third WW in a line of men with the same initials who had all, in their occasionally unorthodox ways, invested in business when venture capital wasn't a career, it was what you did with your family money. William's sage advice: *Treat every presentation like it's a matter of life and death.*

When Emory's turn came for a presentation twelve years later, last on the agenda at the Tuesday morning meeting that William presided over so he could personally screen potential investments before floating the companies to his partners, she did, indeed, steel herself for battle. She was expected to model good presentation skills for the junior staff—and not only sell William on the company that he might later pitch to the partners, but also demonstrate that she had investigated the potential investment inside and out.

Instead of leaning back in her chair, loosening her tie, and folding her hands behind her head, as so many of her male peers did, she took one deep, quiet breath, tilted up her chin, and stood from her rolling conference room chair gracefully. (Rule one of many she'd made after learning the hard way: Never let go of the armrest until you have fully risen or are securely seated, lest you fall on your ass.) She forced her clenched jaw into calm relaxation as she passed by the analysts lining the back wall, where she'd stood herself in the best dress pants and button-down she could afford when she was a new employee, hoping that some of her research would lead to a deal. (Rule two: No nervous smiles or frowns.) She flattened her palm against the side seam of her skirt until she accepted the passing of the projector remote. (Rule three: No visible shaking.) Then she took her place next to the screen, at the far end of the room from where William sat in front of the imposing double doors, so she could easily gesture to her presentation slides.

Battle time. Her left heel was screaming, wounded already— her shopper at Bellworthy's had picked out some perfectly professional nude pumps to go with her new sand-colored skirt suit. She'd worn them around her Brooklyn apartment and they'd seemed fine, so she hadn't ferried them in a separate bag and donned the last bit of her armor at the office.

(Rule four: No wardrobe or grooming distractions.) A small error of strategy. Emory could recover.

She had to. A successful presentation about Neighborhood Answering would crack open the door for two smart, worthy women to get their burgeoning company in front of WW and Partners, and maybe secure an influx of money that would catapult them from startup to wildly successful. It was their dream, and so it was Emory's job to be their trusted ally.

Unfortunately, early April was the worst time to present at the Tuesday hell meeting, no matter how compelling the project at hand, because this season brought slanting sun through the windows and right into her eyes. She took a step in one direction, and then the other, trying to find a place where she could be seen and heard but not have to squint. (Rule five: No obvious discomfort. See also rules two, three, and four.) She *needed* her position at the helm, needed to ensure that William caught every word she floated down over the bagel trays and cups of coffee and folders full of paperwork. Emory turned her head slightly to the side—good enough—and launched into her well-practiced offensive.

By the end of it, she was on a high. The company had a solid team behind it and plenty of growth potential. A note of pride on their behalf crept into her voice. "Ms. Chu and Ms. Nadeem have built their virtual doorman company to scale quickly and efficiently, and they've taken to heart the challenges that plagued earlier companies in the space. They offer a low-cost, high-margin service that's out of reach for the average New Yorker. There will be someone within a few blocks able to check the security cameras or come out in person, around the clock. Someone to answer the buzzer or to watch you safely enter your apartment, even if it's a small building, and even if it's the middle of the night. With the package lockers in apartment lobbies, and the option for apartments to receive regular patrols, and the rest that I've detailed for you, their company can be a one-stop shop for landlords of all sizes who want to increase their security and customer service."

Emory had considered including a few sentences about a time when she'd been followed home to her first apartment, and even practiced those lines down to breaths and silences. In the icy air-conditioning of the conference room, with everyone staring at her, she diverted around the minefield. That story would make her a tasty treat for her peers, and of the five other VPs, four of them would eat her alive if given a good bottle of barbecue sauce. (Rule six: Do not admit any weakness.) There was another gut punch in her presentation's arsenal: protection for wives and daughters and sisters. And using that angle felt like telling girls to not dress like sluts or to not get tipsy and was complete bullshit.

She was stone. (Rule seven, but it was really more of a self-admonition than a rule: Rocks don't sweat.)

The projector remote in her hand was slippery, though. Rocks felt pressure. They had fault lines. Emory didn't want to crack when she had the full attention of the room. But she knew what they wanted to hear. They wanted to hear that they were invincible, and heroically, they could save everyone else. *Wives and daughters.* A false flag operation to draw them in.

But that wasn't her style, no matter how much Emory wanted the room's approval. Instead of speaking aloud the miserable lever about women as victims of crime that she knew—and hated—by heart, she clicked through the next slides of familiar NYC land-marks, mixed in with neighborhoods less familiar to her audience that mostly lived in Manhattan and rarely ventured beyond it. "Because employees will be working in the neighborhoods where they live, Neighborhood Answering will convey a sense of community even while expanding on a national scale. They're set up to start operations in cities in New Jersey and Connecticut next year, and are developing a more focused, concierge-style offering for those in rural areas, in standalone homes, and so on. Other potential lines of business include virtual office services like mail handling and phone lines for small businesses, supporting entrepreneurs who don't need a corporate office space."

Emory pointed out figures in the financial projections and wrapped up her pitch right as the room shifted from paying attention to idly chatting while they flipped through their copies of her deck and the Neighborhood Answering business plan. William was leaned over listening to Tim, another WW and Partners VP. Tim, like all the VPs, was in contention for promotion to junior partner, and they each wanted that coveted, rare opening for themselves. Of course he wouldn't let any opportunity to connect with William pass him by.

Nothing like someone talking over you before you even finish. "Any questions?"

Bryce, who had been a VP since Emory had started at WW and Partners, spoke first. "Not a question, more of a comment. Some of this undercuts coworking spaces and bigger offices. We don't want our real estate partnerships to think we aren't prioritizing them."

Emory did not sigh or roll her eyes. Bryce managed their relationships with several of New York's biggest commercial real estate services. What he didn't have was a sense of scale. "We're not really talking about big firms skipping out on having offices in midtown. The office services are for, say, sole proprietors who never had a corporate headquarters and won't ever need one."

Another VP—Adam Carrington, a nephew of one of the partners who'd made VP nearly five years before anyone else had, and Emory's absolute least favorite colleague—spoke up. "So why don't people move if they're getting packages stolen?" He nudged Bryce. "I mean, if you live in a crappy building with no security in a bad neighborhood, what do you expect?"

The first two years she'd worked at WW and Partners as an intern and then an analyst, Emory lived deep in Queens, where you had to take a bus to get to the subway. Hers wasn't a bad neighborhood; it just wasn't a *great* neighborhood. She'd had her packages delivered to the office during the day and spent her nights chasing down cockroaches. And sure, the minute she'd received a respectable raise she'd moved out. "This is an accessible luxury product for locations where dedicated security staff isn't an option." She flipped back through the slides to the demographic and financial overviews and tried to come up with a response beyond *I'm sorry some people aren't rich enough for you.*

Carrington always activated her *shut up, jerk* instinct. Post-presentation question time was meant to be a chance to catch any oversights, and Carrington's most frequent contribution to the strength testing of investments was proclaiming that if he didn't want something, it was worthless. He ran a hand over his bristly blond crewcut and blathered on. "And won't Chu and Nadeem take the company and run off to Japan or India or wherever? Like, we'll invest and they'll—"

Adam Carrington, worst of the VPs. There was an uncomfortable murmur from the analyst lineup, but not one loud enough to distract Carrington from his smug suppositions. Emory didn't like where this was going. Or what he was implying.

She wondered if he'd say this sort of thing out loud if they weren't both white. Or if the room was more diverse.

The answer was: almost certainly. "Their families are from China and Pakistan, and they were both born here. They're staying."

Fortunately, the bagel tray was circulating, and he stopped putting his foot in his mouth long enough to fill it with carbs. Across the table, Jeff Lieberman, the one VP that Emory actually *did* like, raised his eyebrows in commiseration. She wanted to throw her hands to the ceiling, but that would break the Emory presentation code.

Tim appeared beside her. He'd moved from his right-hand man position at the end of the conference table down to the screen awfully quickly, or she'd been more distracted by Carrington's mouth flatulence than she realized. If Tim had already finished pitching himself to William, something bigger was on his mind.

"Good presentation," Tim said, taking the remote out of her hand. "We need to check on the score now."

Emory looked to the other end of the room for confirmation. William nodded from his presiding position. They'd recently invested in a sports data company, so there was constant gambling talk at the coffee maker.

"Isn't it just an exhibition game today?" she asked, wondering what about a score for a sport she couldn't even remember, on another continent, on a weekday, could matter at that exact moment.

Tim swapped the input over to television. Instead of the game, entertainment news took over the screen. A young, lithe reporter flirted with the camera.

"It's probably blacked out here." Carrington stated the obvious. "So all we're going to get is this garbage." Not even Bryce, the VP who Emory suspected was funneling most of his salary into sports betting, got up and left, though. If they couldn't have sports, they'd take beauty.

Then another beauty appeared on the screen, in tabloid shots of her in a bathing suit, in a clip of her walking down the red carpet, in a scene with her strutting away from an explosion in a form-fitting bodysuit with a cape trailing behind her. She was tall—a smidge over Emory's five feet, ten inches. She could have been Emory's glamourously, spectacularly attractive big sister, with an athletic build, gleaming smile, piercing blue eyes, and bouncy beach-blonde waves.

Emory did not shake. She did not show signs of discomfort. She was making a life and death presentation in the front of the room. *Rocks don't sweat.*

"Marilee Callahan—"

Mari Cooper, Emory's brain insisted.

"—has even more good news. She's not only starting a lifestyle brand, featuring organic nutrition and health products, and her own fitness clothing line—"

Carrington guffawed. "Isn't that your ex, Emory? That chick that dumped you?"

That left me. That rejected me.

That destroyed me.

"—she's starting a brand-new life! Callahan has announced her engagement to her fellow business entrepreneur and tech mogul—

and America's most eligible bachelor—Benjamin Thorston, with the nuptials to be held in Malibu this spring." The screen showed a video of the two of them together at a film premiere. Benjamin Thorston's absurdly pale skin gleamed in the light of paparazzi flashbulbs, but even as strong-jawed and handsome as he was, he couldn't compete with Mari's star-bright smile. She glowed. It was impossible to look away from her.

Emory's ears rang with the unwelcome sounds of immaturity. *Ooh* and *hoo-ee* and *what a woman*. Carrington's whistle was the loudest of all.

"Hey, now," Tim said, grinning at Carrington, who oozed objectification. "Sorry, Emory."

William raised a hand with the benevolence of a man who'd never had to deflect a catcall himself. "That's enough. See if the game is on a different channel."

Tim turned so Emory could see his shit-eating smirk and began flipping through talk shows and infomercials. He avoided her glare. Fortunately for Emory, even the handful of analysts who waited to be dismissed leaned against the back wall and conferred in whispers, or checked their phones, or watched the channel-surfing instead of staring at her. Whatever game they were looking for was a big one.

Emory's phone buzzed in her pocket and she flinched. She thought she'd set it to silent. (Rule eight: Don't interrupt yourself.) With everyone distracted, she pulled it out and pressed her fingertip to the reader on the back. There was a new email from Malibu Elite Weddings, subject line: SAVE THE DATE FOR M... With a shaking hand, she tapped the notification, scrolling through the cordially invited and all the rest to a mid-May date, six weeks in the future.

"We don't get NY Sports Network Four," Tim finally said, pausing on a screen that prompted him to upgrade to a better TV package.

"Then go look on your computers," William said. He didn't use his cell phone for anything but calls, so it did not occur to him that a portion of the room was already tracking down the score that way. "And Emory, you know that actress? Might be the time to get in on the ground floor of her company."

"Yeah, get in with her," Tim muttered.

"I think not getting it in was the whole problem," Carrington whispered to Bryce, who turned his face to the side and giggled.

William either didn't hear or he decided to let the boys be boys. Just like every other time he didn't hear, or he pretended not to hear. "It's a good connection." He gathered his stack of papers. "More importantly, you should connect with Benjamin Thorston. Whatever he's doing next, we want a piece of it. That's the kind of investment that we're looking for. Especially from anyone who wants a promotion." William tucked the papers under his arm and stood to address the room.

"As usual, expect the update on which presentations I'd like to see at the partners meeting by end of day. And, again, Emory, reach out to that"—he nodded his head toward the screen, indicating that he'd forgotten Mari's name already—"woman to get an introduction to Thorston if it's the right time. We're chasing too many mice and not finding enough unicorns." Then he sailed briskly through the double doors of the conference room, officially ending the meeting.

The newest analyst hire, who had the unenviable job of acting as William's executive assistant in addition to his other duties, scurried after. The doors banged closed, which was the unofficial end of the meeting.

"Of course it's the right time," Emory mumbled into the din of scraping chairs and back patting that followed.

Because, despite every cringeworthy comment, despite the long hours and the terrible colleagues, WW and Partners had been loyal to her for twelve years. In those twelve years, WW and Partners hadn't accepted her marriage proposal and then run away to a Hollywood acting career. Mari had done that, eight years ago. *Mari* was the one who didn't want to be partners. Mari was the one who hadn't wanted to fight for her.

It was definitely the right time. The right time to see Mari again. The right time for Emory to show Mari that her heart was *not* still broken.

Not still broken at all.

two

BLISS TULLY WAS LATE TO her appointment in midtown because the F had been stalled between stations for the usual problem: reasons unknown, relayed as a mumble over the loudspeaker. Maybe it was a track fire, or a malfunctioning door, or a broken rail, or a horde of sentient rats. Nobody knew, and that was the fun of it, other than the being late part. She wrestled her granny cart up the stairs and out of the station at Bryant Park, then made her way to a concrete and glass tower that reminded her of childhood visits to her father's office in Connecticut, where she'd sit in a chair in the hallway while he took calls for endless, boring hours and occasionally a secretary would slip her a piece of candy.

At the time, she thought offices were safe places full of good people. She knew better these days.

But that was long ago, and today, she wanted good vibes only. She checked in with the security guard in the lobby and took the elevator up to WW and Partners, the sort of office where a secretary had to buzz you through to a lobby decorated with dark wood and stiff leather wing chairs. And some kind of giant vase that wasn't for flowers, which, in her opinion, was a waste. Waiting anywhere without a good assortment of magazines was also a waste, so Bliss hoped nobody had to wait at WW and Partners very long.

A woman watched her wrestle her granny cart through the heavy glass doors from behind an oversize desk. She had curly dark hair and deep brown skin with copper undertones, and reminded Bliss of a girl she'd had a crush on for a few weeks in fifth grade. Fifth grade, right before everything went to shit. Before her dad—

No. Only good vibes for her today. And for this place, which seemed like it could really, really use a dose of good vibes to combat the *would be comfy like a library if it didn't smell like judgment in here* aesthetic.

That was a meaner thought than Bliss wanted to have running through her brain. She was usually pretty cheerful, but this WW and Partners place was getting to her already. If her new venture was going to survive, she'd have to get over herself, because a lot of offices were like this one.

Like a reminder.

"Are you here for the plants?" the woman asked, setting aside a stack of courier pouches.

Bliss groped in the pocket of her green wool peacoat for a silver case and extracted a business card, then handed it over with a goofy flourish she immediately wished she could take back. "Bliss Tully of Bliss Foliage, at your service. Thanks so much for reaching out." She touched a finger to the name plate on the desk. "Beatriz Reyes?"

Beatriz nodded and offered a wide smile. "Nice to meet another girl with a B name." She quickly and efficiently took Bliss in hand. "You're coming in once a week—"

"Tuesdays and Thursdays to start, but only today this week. After the initial setup, and when the plants are more established, I'll be in once a week on one of those days. Regularly, though! I'll swap out anything that's in bad condition, of course. And if you need extra plants or flowers for an event or for a gift, just let me know, and I'll bring those in for you. I'm here to make things beautiful." Bliss took a breath. She hadn't practiced her spiel out loud, or even in her head, and it had come out a lot faster than she'd expected.

Beatriz held up her phone and snapped a photo. "I'll add you to the security list for both of those days as a vendor, and they'll have a permanent pass for you next time you come. Unless you already have another client in the building?"

Bliss shook her head. "Nope." She pressed her lips into a tight smile so that she wouldn't say what Beatriz didn't need to know: WW and Partners was her first, and presently her only, Bliss Foliage client. That the business card she'd handed over so casually was the lone piece of collateral in her inventory and she had printed it at home last night. And all of this was a big, big problem.

Good vibes.

Beyond the wall behind Beatriz's desk, which divided the WW and Partners lobby from a corridor, sharp-suited men streamed by. A few swaggered past importantly while touching a Bluetooth headset and talking a little too loudly, except for one who reminded Bliss of an overgrown puppy. He made the time for a wave as he bustled past. "Hi, Beatriz!"

"Hey Jeff, say hi to the kids! And to Melody!" Beatriz pushed a diagram of the office across her desk and bent over it with Bliss. "Here's where you can hang your coat. Big conference room at the end of the hall, CEO all the way down on the other side. On that far end are senior employee offices and a couple of small meeting rooms, and back down here by the big conference room, there are a few more small rooms, some cubicles for the newbies, and some junior employee offices. In the middle is the kitchen and the supply room. Those don't need any plants." She looked up at Bliss and deliberately tapped the cubicles. When she was sure Bliss was watching, she circled them again with a finger. "Please prioritize the senior employee spaces."

Bliss grinned and a good portion of the tension in her shoulders disappeared. Vibe check: better than expected. There wouldn't be a lot of room in the cubicles for pots, but as a former windowless cubicle dweller, she knew that even a little bit of green could make things feel a lot sunnier under the fluorescent lights. She took the diagram and a pencil that Beatriz offered, ready to make notes. "I think we're on the same page."

Twenty minutes later, with a repurposed art apron fastened over her all-black but not quite *matching* black outfit, she'd had a look at the boardroom, passed by a line of small meeting rooms with no natural light at all, and offered tiny pots of bamboo and pothos to the workers in the block of cubicles that indicated their lowly position in the company. Most of them seemed suspicious until she said the plants were a "Company perk!" and then they claimed their pots immediately.

Out of the corner of her eye, when she was checking her too-pale face in the reflection of a darkened office window, she caught a reedy man in thick glasses whispering softly to his new bamboo. Bringing some small plants along had been a last-minute decision; her plan for the day was to get the lay of the corporate land and then bring in what the office needed.

Her heart was full. She'd made her own good vibe.

Bliss left a few more bamboo pots on empty desks and ventured back down the corridor. It turned a corner, and while the inner side of the hall was more of the small meeting rooms, closets, and HVAC panels, the outer edge was lined with tiny offices that featured both walls and doors, and to Bliss's relief, windowsills. She stepped into each and took notes on the light and which way the windows faced. The offices got bigger as she went along, and though all were nicely furnished, none was so nice as the CEO's—an airy, palatial space, signaling the apex of the company hierarchy.

Her father had had an office like this one, designed to intimidate by its size alone. You thought these kinds of offices were nice at first, but the people who worked in them always did you dirty.

The empty offices were creepy. Time to get moving.

She worked her way back down the hall, dropping off an aloe in one office and a sago palm in another. Her granny cart was almost empty; she'd found spots for almost everything she'd brought along, and she hadn't had anything for more than half of the individual offices. There was a single plant left, and she decided to leave it in a tiny, bright office halfway down the line of seniority.

Unlike some of the other offices, the one she'd chosen didn't have any family photos or golf trophies on the windowsill, so there was plenty of room for a plant for its occupant: Emory Jordan, Vice-President. Bliss had the perfect thing—well, she only had one thing. She gingerly removed a potted cactus, an *Echinocereus stramineus*, from the bottom of her cart. She'd found the strawberry hedgehog cactus at a street fair three years ago, the size of a tiny button, and it had grown into a decent burrito. Twice since then it had outgrown its pot and currently lived in a bright pink planter. It was *cute*.

Two steps into the room, she heard "Excuse me," and she spun to explain herself—and when she did, she smashed full on into an intimidatingly attractive woman. A woman who sent a chill of rightness through her, a woman whose presence stilled the world for a moment.

But not for long enough. Bliss rammed right into her arm.

With the cactus.

The woman stared at Bliss, betrayal etching her features. She clapped a hand over her arm, which was riddled with little spines, and let out a yelp. "What the—"

"Don't touch those!" Bliss cast around and then deposited the cactus on the floor. She wanted to kick it under the desk and pretend it never existed. "You'll make it worse. Let me help you."

"How do I know *you* won't make it worse?" the woman snapped.

Bliss brought her palms together in supplication. "I am truly sorry, and I promise I know how to make it better right now."

There was a particular kind of woman who went to the gym and drank fresh-squeezed juice and ran the world that Bliss had a weakness for, and Bliss was feeling that weakness for the woman with long, honey-blonde hair that cascaded over her shoulders and bright, intelligent hazel eyes. For one perfect moment, Bliss had been sure that she and this towering goddess of a woman were *supposed* to collide. But they definitely weren't supposed to collide like *this*.

"I can't even reach the cactus from here, so I definitely can't make it worse." She patted her apron pocket like it would deliver something to save the day. "Do you happen to have tweezers?"

The woman dropped her suit jacket and a stack of folders into one of the chairs in front of the desk—probably *her* desk, Bliss realized. The good vibes dissipated. "I am so sorry, so, so sorry, I didn't expect anyone to come in, I..."

The woman shouldered past Bliss to sit in the empty guest chair. She pulled a briefcase out from under the desk and searched through it one-handed. Bliss watched her balance the bag on her knees, where her legs stretched long. The woman's pantyhose was a light sand color, the same shade as her skin. Her suit was a terribly boring dust-colored jacket and skirt, and her stiletto heels were matte beige, with only a sleeveless white shell to break up the monochrome palette. Not that Bliss objected. *She looks good in nude.*

She forced the thought away. Most women weren't interested in other women. Especially not when a meet-cute was a meet-mutilation. And a woman who worked in a place like this was part of the hands-off club. She was pretty on the outside, but corporate work practically guaranteed her inside was all asshole.

The woman held up a pair of tweezers and put her bag aside. "Now what?"

Bliss carefully moved the stack of papers and the jacket from the other seat to the desk, watching for any objection, then balanced gingerly on the edge of the chair. She took the tweezers and put one hand under the woman's wrist so she could see the damage.

"Ouch."

There was no missing the eyebrow that arched up. "Yes, I noticed."

"Okay, hold still. This shouldn't be too bad. It would have been a lot worse if the spines had been smaller, because they'd have been harder to see and to pull out." She plucked one as gently as she could and dropped it into the trashcan. "How was that?"

She got a shrug. That was workable. It wasn't enough of a distraction to last through the rest of the spines. Bliss would have to make conversation. "Um, is this your office? You're Vice-President Emory?"

The woman—Emory—nodded warily. Bliss went on. "I'm Bliss. I can be Lissie or Liss. Only my mom calls me that, though. I'm just saying that you can call me whatever you want."

Emory surprised her. "I want you to be whoever you already are."

Bliss extracted another spine. Emory's arm was supple and shapely, and she smelled like fresh air. How anyone smelled like fresh air in midtown Manhattan was beyond Bliss's comprehension. Technically everyone should have smelled like exhaust and garbage juice. "I want to be Bliss, then." Emory opened and squeezed her hand a few times before letting it go limp. Maybe Bliss's nervous talking was working magic. "What do you do here in this stuffy office?" Maybe that was the wrong sort of nervous talking. Besides, she didn't really care what Emory did. The leather and wood and snobby signage told her everything she needed to know about who worked at WW and Partners.

"I'd like to point out that you're also in this stuffy office." The desk phone rang, and Emory hit a button that silenced it. She watched Bliss take out another spine and hissed softly. "I go to stuffy meetings. I pitch businesses to the company, and if I'm successful, I get to help make businesses better. We advise businesses and give them money, and then when they get bigger, they give the money back with profit. Or we keep owning part of the business, maybe. Lots of possibilities."

"Oh?" Bliss rubbed her finger over the spot where a spine had been, feeling for anything she'd missed. "So you make businesses successful."

"Sometimes. Sometimes you fail. A lot of the time, at my level, you fail. And it's one thing when you fail because you got beat, but it's another thing entirely when you fail because nobody believes in you."

A deep frown crossed her face and Bliss held the tweezers still. A look like that didn't come from a cactus spine. There was something else going on. A couple of employees passed down the hall, and Bliss could hear their laughter—a "hur, hur, hur" that eventually faded when a door slammed shut. Emory got her feet beneath herself and pushed herself up straight in her chair. "But that's business."

The phone rang again and Emory picked up with her free hand. "Hello, Clark, can I call you right back? I'm in the middle of something, but in a few minutes, I'll be able to give you my full attention. Thanks so much."

There were three big spines left. Bliss needed Emory to be distracted a little longer. "How do you get into a place like this? Like, how do you start working here?"

"Lucked into it during school." Emory was quiet while Bliss twisted her arm back and forth, examining the angle of the spines so she could pull them out with minimal damage. Emory repeated the question back. "How did *you* get into a place like this?"

Bliss removed the last spine and pulled Emory's arm close to inspect her work. Her own distraction let the truth slip. "I sent postcards to every business in a ten-block radius. Beatriz was the one person who called."

Emory leaned forward. "That's good. Good for you." Her hazel gaze was curious. And seated, without the additional advantage of three-inch heels, she wasn't so intimidating. Her hair slipped down over her shoulder, so close Bliss wanted to touch the soft curve at the end and curl it around and around her finger. "Thanks. You have good hands, Bliss."

The spines had probably hurt a lot, but Bliss was the one feeling tortured. She did have good hands. If Emory only knew.

A second later, Bliss remembered that people like Emory couldn't be trusted. She felt like she was on some third-rate carnival ride, bouncing back and forth while her brain rattled out of her head. She dropped Emory's arm. "If you have anything like witch hazel or aloe, that would be good to put on later. There's an aloe plant in another office down the hall—I left one. I think it said Adam Carrington on the door?"

Emory raised her face to the ceiling and huffed out a long breath.

Bliss didn't know what to make of that. "Go to the doctor if your arm gets puffy or hot, or if it keeps hurting." She scooped up the cockeyed cactus and carried it tenderly to the windowsill. It had been through a lot.

Emory pushed in the extra chairs and settled herself behind her desk while Bliss used a corner of her apron to right the plant in its pot, and when she did, she noticed a tiny prism hung on a metal rod. She'd completely forgotten that was there. When she pulled her apron away, the prism caught the sun and scattered rainbows across her front. "Should I—"

"That's the most fun this stuffy office has seen in a while." A rainbow streak refracted on the wall behind Emory's computer monitor. It was the brightest spot in all of WW and Partners. "Might not be the right accessory for all of the offices, though."

Bliss nodded. *Good business advice.* "I will check on your cactus next week. We can see if you want to stick with it or not."

"Stick with it," Emory repeated. She snorted. An endearing little snort, angry-cute like—like a strawberry hedgehog cactus. The side of her mouth twitched, then twitched again, and the start of Emory's smile disappeared.

Was it the pun? Was that smile a crack in the ice? Bliss edged toward the door anyway.

"Next week. We'll see if I'm feeling prickly then," Emory said.

Bliss laughed.

And fled.

calhounhoward.com